MATCHMAKER

LAUREN LANDISH

D1115882

Edited by VALORIE CLIFTON
Edited by STACI ETHERIDGE
Photography by ALEX WIGHTMAN

MATCHMAKER

BY LAUREN LANDISH

30 men. 1 woman.

I know how it sounds… **dirty**.

Except it's just the premise for a new reality show,
Matchmaker, where I'm supposed to find love on TV.

Thirty sexy eligible bachelors are competing for my hand,
trying to prove their love for me in front of millions of
people.

I know most are fake and only here to advance their careers,
but there are two who draw me to them like a moth to
a flame.

One is blond and blue-eyed, with a chiseled body and a
prowling natural grace. And while he might seem a little
rough around the edges, with me, he's kind and genuine.

The other is passionate, driven, and totally focused on me–everything a woman could want.

I feel so torn. Do I choose the one I'm falling in love with, or can I be happy settling for the safe bet?

That should be an easy question. If I were a bystander sitting at home, I know what my answer would be.

But I'm scared. He could destroy me, burn me to ash with his fire. And if I'm wrong about him, I don't know if I'll ever recover...

Join my mailing list and receive 2 FREE ebooks! You'll also be the first to know of new releases, sales, and giveaways.

Irresistible Bachelor **Series (Interconnecting standalones):**
Anaconda ‖ Mr. Fiance ‖ Heartstopper
Stud Muffin ‖ Mr. Fixit ‖ Matchmaker
Motorhead ‖ Baby Daddy

PROLOGUE

EMILY

y knees are weak, shaking beneath the length of my formal gown as I stare blankly at the pops of color across the dark night sky. Behind me, I can feel a faint wind tickle my exposed back, making the fountain show a little blurry as the lights flash on the moving water sprays. I'm sure it's spectacular, but I don't even really see it. I try to blink, focus on something, anything, but I'm lost in some sort of weird hypnotic trance. My arms feel heavy, and it's only the waving motion of the producer off camera that snaps me out of it.

The two men across from me are both strikingly handsome, but that's where the similarities end. One is blond and blue-eyed, with a chiseled body and a prowling natural grace. And while he might seem a little rough around the edges, with me, he's kind and genuine. The other is the epitome of tall, dark, and handsome. He has a way with words that makes me feel precious.

If there's anything these two men have in common, it's the

look in their eyes, one of equal parts want and need. But is it real? How can I be sure?

This is my deciding moment, and I feel so torn. Do I choose the one I'm falling in love with, the one who pushes me and lights flames deep in my soul? That should be an easy question, and if I were a bystander sitting at home on my couch, I'd readily say yes. But I'm scared. He could destroy me, burn me to ash with his fire. And if I'm wrong about him, I don't know if I'll ever recover.

People are pulling me the other way, telling me the other guy is the better choice and backing that up with good reasons. The other guy is passionate, driven, and totally focused on me. He's everything a woman could want. But my heart doesn't flutter when I think about him. Can I be happy settling for safe?

It's all just happening so fast. I only met them a few weeks ago, and it's been a whirlwind of romantic adventures ever since. Admittedly, most of it has been orchestrated by the show, contrived by the people behind the camera who have walked me step by step through the journey to this moment.

So whom do I chose?

"Emily!" the producer calls, obviously exasperated with my unintentional overly dramatic pause. "We don't have time to stand around all night. I need the choice before the light show finishes!"

I take a deep breath, trying not to lose my lunch all over my high heels. I give a nod and count to five, pausing as I see flickers of emotion in the eyes of both men.

Fear. Uncertainty. I know exactly how they feel.

Even though I'm not sure how this is going to end, I dutifully begin. "I've thought long and hard about this, so gentlemen, let's see if we're a Match. Please . . . turn over your cards."

"I still can't believe it!" I cry into the phone to my friend Cassie as I walk out of my bathroom, fresh out of the shower and over the moon giddy. "They really want me!"

"We've been over this. You'd better believe it, girl!" Cassie laughs. I'm sure she's happy it's finally become a reality for me as I've annoyed her to death ever since I sent my video to the producers. "Unless you've suddenly become grotesque or killed a man, they picked you. You've sailed through all their Q-and-A sessions, and I'm guessing you've haven't had a zit pop up overnight, so you're golden. It's you, babe."

I've been running around my room like a chicken with its head cut off, but at Cassie's words, I pause and squeal, "O.M.G. It's so happening! Hollywood, here I come!"

"Congrats again!" Cassie exclaims. "I'm so happy for you!" She adds under her breath, "Thank you, Jesus! I don't have to listen to 'I wonder if they think I'm cute enough' over and over anymore."

I can't stop smiling, my heart soaring to the heavens. "I know, right? I mean, after I sent in my video, I was convinced I wouldn't get a call back. They must get thousands of submissions from interesting women. Me? I'm regular old Emily, nothing special.

"You are special!" Cassie says. "I know it, you know it, and they damn sure know it or they wouldn't have picked you. Now, serious question here . . . you got your outfits picked yet?"

I can hear the grin in her voice as she asks, and I nod, even though she can't see me. "Yeah, a few. They told me that I only needed to bring a few spare outfits and they would provide the rest."

"Damn, they're just rolling out the red carpet for you, aren't they?" Cassie jokes. "Sure they have one wide enough?"

"My carpet's a lot skinnier than yours, Miss Future Real Estate Mogul," I say, casually tossing back her dig. Furrowing my brow, I bite my lower lip thoughtfully. "I'm just dying to know what the show is going to be about. The ad was attached to the season finale of *Survivor*, but the execs told me it would be something totally different." Thinking about it, my mind goes back to when I first got the call.

"Hello, this is Meredith Ward of Ward-Williams Productions. I wanted to talk to you about your video submission," the business-woman announces when I pick up the phone.

I almost hang up on the spot. Just another attempt by Cassie at playing a prank on me. No way they're calling me.

"Nice joke, Cass! You're not fooling me!"

The laughter at the other end of the line tells me that I'm way off. God, I'm such an idiot. Her laughter assures me that I didn't ruin my chance. "Miss Parks, I assure you this is no joke, and the only Cass I know is a seven-foot-tall guy."

"Oh, my God, I'm so sorry!" I spew, blushing furiously. "Miss . . .? I'm an idiot."

"Meredith Ward. And relax. I just want to chat a little. Your video caught our attention."

I try to keep my racing heartbeat under control as she begins to ask questions that are mostly about me. Where I grew up, why I love working with kids, and why I applied to the show. I try to answer them honestly without running on forever. I don't want to sound like a ditzy airhead. She seems especially interested to know if I have any skeletons in the closet, explaining that the show's producers don't want any shockers while the show is on air. I don't blame them. Scandals have been known to sink ratings like a ninety-year-old's tits.

She laughs politely when I tell her the worst thing I'd ever done was steal a lollipop as a kid, but I took it back before I even made it down the block. "Well, Emily, I have to say that I've got a few more calls to make, but I like your chances."

Since then, I've talked to Meredith several more times, including a Skype interview with a panel of show executives. They already knew the answers to all the questions they asked me, since Meredith had already asked them before. They probably just wanted to see my reaction, but I answered in the same way I did with her—truthfully and honestly.

I'm still not sure what I've gotten myself into. It's all hush-hush, and no one will say a word. You'd think it was a top-secret government program.

"Well, as long as it's not one of those shows where you'll be one of many helpless women chasing one ding-a-ling belonging to the biggest douchebag ever, all while begging him to choose you to be his love interest after he's probably fucked all the other girls, then I think you'll be all right," Cassie says, breaking me out of my reverie.

I let out a laugh. "Oh, hell no. This might be my dream, but I do have my limits. I have class and standards, I'll have you know."

"Could've fooled me," Cassie quips. "Not sure 'class and standards' apply to a girl who will babysit one night and then dance on a pole the next."

"Hey! That was one night. You dared me, and may I remind you that I took second place?" I growl. "Don't hate."

Cassie laughs, and I can't help but smile despite my nerves about being in the dark on what I'm getting into.

I glance at my clock. "Crap!" I say. "I've gotta go! The production limo will be here soon."

"Production limo? To your house?" Cassie asks, sounding shocked. "Girl, what are you not telling me?"

"I'm as surprised as you. They said something about Cinderella treatment, something I wouldn't know the least bit about. But I can't argue with that!"

"I don't blame you, but you be safe, you hear? Call me when you get there. I'm dying to know what this is about."

"I am too. And I will," I promise. "Bye, babe."

"Details! I want all the details!" Cassie yells as I pull my phone away, making me chuckle. I hang up the phone and scurry over to the closet. I don't have much time to get ready. I need to be quick. Flipping through clothes, I rummage through my wardrobe, trying on different outfits with the speed of Wonder Woman. Meredith said to wear something nice, but I don't know what that means. Finally, I settle on a body-hugging red dress that makes my eyes pop. I don't remember where I got it, but as soon as I saw it, I had to have it. It's like it carries good luck or something. And it's decidedly nicer than my usual lazy-chic jeans and tees.

Staring at my reflection in the mirror, I don't think I look bad at all. With bra-length blonde hair, blue eyes, and hips that give me an hourglass figure, I look like the modern girl next door. Maybe that's why they chose me. But what they plan to do with me, I have no idea.

Flashing myself a wink, I gather my purse and a tiny duffel bag of belongings. I'm not even outside for a minute before a shiny black limo pulls up. Out of the corner of my left eye, I can see my nosy neighbor Ethel Crabtree perched on her porch, nearly falling out of her rocking chair to get a view of what's going on. And to my right, wannabe real housewife Holly Vereen is just pulling into her driveway and getting out of her SUV. She's dressed in a black knockoff Versace jumpsuit, her mouth falling open when she sees the limo driver jump out to serve me.

"Emily!" she gasps in surprise, gawking at the limo. "What's all this about?"

I flash her a grin, trying not to laugh as the driver motions inside the vehicle. "If you'll please, Miss Parks."

Holly usually ignores me and sticks her nose up at me whenever I try to speak to her, so I find it hilarious that she wants my attention now. "Sorry, Mrs. Vereen, but I don't have time to chat," I respond cheerfully, giving her a friendly wave. "You have a wonderful day!"

"But—" she begins to protest, but her words are lost as I dip into the limo and the driver closes the door.

I'm immediately enveloped in luxury, sitting back against the leather seats. I let out a low whistle as I look around at all the finery. This thing is equipped with everything, even a bar and a popup flat-panel TV.

I can hardly stop gawking. It's all so much. As someone who's lived a working class life, I've never been in a limo or a car this decked out before. Running my hands over the supple leather seats, I can hardly believe what's happening. This almost feels like a dream.

As the driver pulls away from the sidewalk, I can see Holly rushing over to gossip with Ethel through the tinted windows. Both of them are staring with wide eyes, gesturing wildly at the limo. I know they're talking about me, wondering what in the world is going on, but they're quickly forgotten as we leave the street and the two women and my house disappear from view.

As we move through the city, my mind returns to my Skype interview with the show's producers.

"Emily, you know that you will be in isolation during filming, correct?"

I'm sitting in my living room, nervous as I look into the camera. I nod, hoping they don't see me twisting the hell out of the washcloth in my lap. "Yes. Meredith explained it to me."

"She's got a good voice. Teeth aren't too horsey," someone else says as the group begins talking about me like I'm not even there. Some say I'm perfect, and others comment like I'm some prize pedigree at a dog show.

"We should get the dynamic duo on her," another producer says.

"They can do something about that skin and her hair."

"Oh, and make sure we get her measurements. I want to reduce that hippiness that's going to show up on-screen," someone says, and I'm beginning to feel like a reject from the dog pound. Seriously, bitch? Hippy?

"We'll take care of all that," Meredith says. "Just remember, Emily, we might sound cruel, but this is going to be a once-in-a-lifetime adventure. We'll be in touch soon."

Damn, she had to say that last line. I'm hooked again.

"Miss Parks?"

I look up, realizing I've been lost in thought. "Sorry. Yes?"

"We're at the airport." The driver lets me out, and I quickly go through security and board the plane. First class, something I can certainly get used to. On the flight over to LAX, I try to sleep, but I'm so nervous I can't keep my eyes closed. I have no clue what awaits me at my final destination. I'm supposed to 'find out when I get there'.

When we touch down, I'm a ball of nerves and I have to drag myself through the airport to my waiting ride—another decked-out limo. It's chaos as we pull out of the terminal into bumper-to-bumper traffic, but I relax against my seat as I peer out the tinted windows. We make our way to the congested highway and the crowded, seemingly never-ending urban landscape.

Los Angeles. The City of Angels. Some people call it the city of sinners, but I really don't know anything about all that. As a small-town girl, I'm taken aback at the enormity of the place. It's HUGE. And the traffic is insane. I swear it seems like hours since we left LAX, yet we probably haven't even gone five miles. Thankfully, the limo is comfy and I can sip at a mineral water as we crawl along.

Apparently, we're headed to Beverly Hills, a place where I hear mansions are a dime a dozen and being rich is the natural way of life. After what seems like an eternity, we finally make it through traffic driving well outside the city into an area where the houses are appropriately called estates and the rolling hills are truly golden mini-kingdoms.

My chest tightens with anxiety as we finally slow down, pulling up in front of a wrought-iron gate. After a moment, it slowly swings open and we move forward again. That's when I see the mansion, the air fleeing from my lungs.

A big circular drive surrounds an architectural marble foun-tain, tall windows cover the front facade, and there are unusual blocks of stucco popping out of the sections of design. The effect is one of sleek contemporary luxury like nothing I've ever seen.

The driver jumps out and opens my door, helping me out of the opulent cabin. I'm not even on my feet long enough to admire the gorgeous estate before a harried looking guy dressed in black slacks, a white dress shirt, and square black glasses rushes up to me.

"Emily?" he asks, giving me a cursory lookover and then offering his hand as I nod. "I'm Nate, Meredith's assistant."

I take his hand, flashing a friendly but nervous smile. "Nice to meet you, Nate—"

"Let's get you inside. They're waiting on you," he says, cutting me off and turning away.

My heart pounds in my chest as my anxiety rises. "Oh, sorry . . . am I late?"

Nate turns and looks at me, smiling sarcastically. "Well aren't you polite? No, you're not late. We're just on a timeline. Move it, toots."

Okaaaaay. Looks like I'm going to have to exercise my behavioral skills I reserve for misbehaving children. That is, if I don't want to end up going off and ruining whatever this is.

I know this is Hollywood and that things work and move differently here. But damn, have some manners.

Don't complain now. You always wanted to know what it was like to see how things were behind the scenes. Now you'll get to find out.

I keep my smile plastered on my face as Nate speed-walks into the house. I try to keep up through a twist and turn of hallways and two flights of stairs, but I find myself having to jog or risk getting left behind. By the time we make it to where we're going, I'm nearly out of breath.

Rapping on a huge frosted glass door once, Nate slides it open, inviting me in with a wave of his arms. Before I can say a word, he's shut the door behind him with a whispered, "Good luck, toots."

Silence envelops me and my skin pricks as my eyes fall on the group of people seated at a large table in front of me. I look from face to face, my heart pounding like a battering ram. I recognize several from the Skype call, but there's a few new faces too, and almost none of them look happy to see me.

They're staring at me. Hard. The silence is so thick, I swear they can hear my heart beating out of my chest. Finally, someone speaks. "Well, she isn't just a photo-only star."

"That dress is horrendous, though. What is that, five years ago?"

"I'd say seven. But Wardrobe can work that out."

The comments go on, leaving me feeling like a side of beef again before an impeccably dressed woman with a sharp grey side-bob rises to her feet and silence drops over everyone. I recognize her immediately. Meredith. She walks around the table, her heels clicking against the hardwood floor, and fixes a friendly smile on her face.

"Emily, my dear," she greets in a no-nonsense voice. She might be trying to sound friendly, but I suspect she eats baby seals for breakfast with the ice she's got in her eyes. "So good to see you again. I trust your flight was excellent." She pauses dramatically, as if waiting for my response.

Not trusting myself to speak, I softly nod, trying to calm myself.

Her smile grows wider and she gestures to a chair on the opposite side of the table. There's a stack of papers in front of it. "Please, have a seat. We have a lot of ground to cover." The tone of her voices makes it clear that I'm not to interrupt and any questions are simply rhetorical.

I sit as commanded, looking at the stack of papers. It looks like I'm about to sign my entire life away. "Uh . . . what is all this?"

Meredith glances at the group of men and women, a silent exchange passing through them. Then she turns around and claps her hands. "Ah, yes. First . . . contracts. We'll need you to sign stating that you are, in fact, who you say you are and the information you provided in all interviews and paperwork is true and complete. We don't want any surprises." Her voice drops low on the last sentence. A part of me feels slightly disappointed. I'm a woman of my word and I told them I had no secrets. But I have to remind myself that she doesn't really know me. Who knows how many people have said the same thing but then turned out to be anything but?

I stare at the contract for a moment, my heart still pounding. I was sent mock copies to go over before I came, but now that the real deal is right in front of me, it feels surreal.

Sweat beads my brow as I feel the weight of eyes on me, and I quickly scribble my signature on the dotted lines on each page that requires my name.

When I'm done, Meredith gestures and someone takes the papers and slides some more in front of me. "Next is the NDA. What we're sharing today and what will occur throughout filming is all hush-hush until after the season airs and promotions are complete." She taps the table. "Sign."

I gulp as I look down at the dotted line. But there is no use fretting. I came all this way. No way I can leave without finding out the details.

I quickly sign the next few pages, and for the next fifteen minutes, it seems to go on and on. Waivers and contracts, agreements for media usage, licensing of my image—I have an image? On and on and on until I feel like I'm on autopilot.

When I get to the one agreeing to be on the show, I pause, something occurring to me. "Before I sign this last one," I say, a moment of clarity striking in the whirlwind of papers, "can you finally tell me what this is going to be about?"

I swear I'm going to wilt under Meredith's stern gaze, but I hold steady. She had to expect it. Who'd sign everything without even knowing what they're committing to?

Meredith exchanges glances with the producers. They each silently look at each other, long, dramatic pauses that draw out the moment long enough to make me want to pull out my hair and scream.

Finally, they come to a silent consensus. Meredith gives me a warm smile, proudly announcing, "The show will be the hottest new reality show. We're honored for you to become our first matcher."

I frown in confusion. "A matcher?"

Meredith's smile grows wider. "Yes. The show will be a romance format. You know, like *The Bachelorette*? Similar, but our version is going to be called *Matchmaker*."

CHAPTER 2

HAYDEN

"Move your arm down just a little," the photographer orders as several blinding shots go off in my face. Frances is a skinny French guy with a bald head and hawk eyes. He pauses once, motioning at me with a hurried gesture.

Moving my hand down my stomach, I do as he says, all while trying to keep my pose. I'm wearing a towel balanced precariously around my waist, so there's not much to it, but I'm careful not to let it fall. Something tells me Frances would like that a little too much.

"Yesss, yesss," he hisses admirably in his French accent, moving around me like a snake and snapping multiple shots. "Perfect . . . pretty boy."

I ignore him and zone out the sound of his voice, keeping my facial expression frozen and hard. He talks too much for my taste and seems to dig my physique in a way that makes me slightly uncomfortable. But it's nothing I haven't dealt with before. I just want to hurry up and get this over with.

For the second time today, I wonder how I ended up here, doing modeling jobs for second-rate labels. I had everything going for me in high school. I was practically destined for the big leagues. Everyone was convinced that I'd be the next big thing, the next baseball legend. Then the unexpected happened. A long fly ball, an outfield fence that was a little too low, a bad landing . . . and I was sidelined by an injury that wiped away my dreams of a sports scholarship to play ball. But a chance encounter with a scout a few years ago got me out of my small town, which was the real goal anyway, so I guess posing for some pictures isn't all that bad. It's damn sure not baseball though.

I swallow, clenching my jaw and forcing away the memory. I hate thinking about it. It just pisses me off and sets me off my game.

For my photoshoot, we're using an abandoned building that looks like it went through World War II with stripped walls and dilapidated architecture.

There's dust and debris strewn across the floor here and there throughout the large room, leftover remnants of a wall that was torn out, and gang graffiti was spray-painted on the wall behind me. But the worst part about it is the smell. It smells dank and musty, like the local bums come here to piss their drunkenness away. I'm having a hard time keeping a straight face through it all.

It definitely isn't a spot that I would've chosen for the shoot, but it's not like I really have a say in the matter. I shoot where they want me to shoot most of the time. Besides, posing in front of graffiti in a rundown warehouse is supposedly edgy and plays into the sexy bad boy image that I usually get booked for. Guess that's what happens when you're jacked, inked, and wear an aura of cockiness like a favorite leather jacket.

"Perfect!" Frances exclaims, smiling at me and then gesturing again. "Now turn around just a little and show me some of your butt." I don't like his tone, but I'm professional. Besides, a little top of the ass was agreed upon before the shoot. I start to do as he says, but then he adds, "And hook your thumbs in the front of the towel to lower it. Show a smidge of hair and the base of your cock."

I freeze. That wasn't part of the agreement. "No. Dick pics aren't in the contract and you damn well know it."

Frances's eyebrows lift up and he seems surprised I'm not just doing what he says without a second thought, probably accustomed to people jumping anytime he demands. But I just stare back at him as he blows up, ranting about how he knows what sells better than some asshole model who thinks he's hot shit.

What the fuck am I doing? I'm not a damn porn star. Fuck this.

I walk over and grab my jeans and t-shirt, not saying a word. I pull my jeans up while Frances gawks at me and I think he's still looking at my ass. As he realizes I'm actually leaving, his tirade continues. I'm pretty sure he even tells me to fuck myself in French as I slip my t-shirt over my head, but I can't be sure.

His voice only gets louder as I walk off. "You know what I can't stand about models like you?" Frances demands. "You think because you're good-looking that you're owed the world. Well, news flash. Hot men like you are a dime a dozen. You're nothing special. Hell, the last model I shot was far cuter than you." He pauses for a moment, then adds, "Maybe you can book a Dad Bod gig next time."

I stop in my tracks, my back to him, and I smile. Now I know he's full of shit, but it's not worth making this situation worse.

I wait till I'm on the street before calling my agent, Jay Coleman.

"Yo?" Jay answers in his customary greeting.

"What the fuck, Jay?" I growl. Jay's been my agent for the past few years when he discovered me after my injury. We've gotten pretty close, and we're never formal when we speak. "You sending me on soft porn shoots now or something?"

"What the hell are you talking about?" Jay asks in confusion.

"He wanted to see my dick!" I hiss. Right as I say 'dick', an old lady walks by and shoots me a dirty look, forcing me to lower my voice. I wait till she passes before I continue. "He was already giving me weird vibes even before that. I walked out on him."

Jay laughs. "Dude, I'm sure he didn't want to see your Full Monty. It was for the chicks."

"I don't know about that man," I say, remembering the way Frances looked at me. "Not what I signed up for either way."

Jay lets out a sigh. "I really wish you wouldn't have walked off set like that . . ." his voice trails off, but I get the point. Maybe he's right. Maybe it was just a little tease for the ladies. But my mom buys every single ad I do and shows it to all of her book club friends. Talk about fucking awkward. Fuck it. It's over now.

"It's too late now. It's over and done with. You got anything else for me?" I ask.

Jay pauses as if he's going to scold me further for my fallout with Frances, but then his tune changes. "Yeah, I do, actually, but it's a stretch. Some new TV show is doing auditions. Could be a good opportunity for some screen time if you make it."

I grunt scornfully. "Seriously? Jay, you know I can't act for shit. What the hell would I do on a TV show?"

"No, not just any TV show," Jay says with growing excitement in his voice that makes me nervous. "Reality TV."

"Oh, fuck that, that's even worse." I hate reality TV. The most I've ever watched was a couple of seasons of *Survivor* when it first started. Anything else I've seen in passing made me want to gouge my fucking eyeballs out. Bunch of grade-A douchebags if you ask me. And the chicks weren't much better.

Jay presses. "Oh, come on, dude, it could actually be perfect for you. No real acting. Flash those dimples, flex your biceps, flip your hair, and I bet you're a shoe-in." When I don't reply, Jay adds, "Just think, it'll be great exposure!"

I scratch at the fresh stubble on my jaw. I still don't like the idea, but I don't really have many options right now. Fuck my life. "I . . . I'll think about it."

There's a long pause on Jay's end, a pause I recognize almost instantly. "Jay," I say slowly, feeling a sense of dread, "what did you do?"

Jay coughs. "So yeah, I kind of already submitted your head-shots along with a video profile from the agency."

"What the fuck—" I begin to yell but stop when a woman with her kid walks by. She speeds up as she passes, bending over to whisper something in her son's ear.

"And they called this morning to invite you for an audition," Jay says, stunning me into silence. "Congratulations?"

It takes me a moment to recover my voice. "Dude, are you serious? You just pimp me out without even running it by me?"

"Yeah, I did," Jay says, a firm note entering his voice. "I'm your agent. That's my goddamn job. And with you just walking out on this gig, a little thanks could be in order."

"I hate when you do this," I growl.

"Stop whining and get your shit together," Jay says. "I'll text you the info now. And by the way, you're welcome."

Click.

I stare at my phone for a moment as the sounds of bustling traffic fill my ears. A part of me wants to call Jay back and chew him out, but the other part of me realizes he's right. He's just doing his job.

With no jobs on the horizon, this new gig might be mandatory. Maybe I just need to give it a try and make the most of it. What do I have to lose? And maybe I can get some face time, get something out of it.

"Guess I'm auditioning for a reality TV show."

CHAPTER 3

EMILY

"Y ou'll have to remember, a lot of these guys are here for their own personal reasons," Meredith says as I sit before her in a room that looks like it might be used for filming in one way or another with all the props. The flow of the room is somewhat ruined by the millions of wires running across the floor, hooked up to several different cameras. "Chances are slim that any will have actual real feelings for you, but they'll pretend that you're the greatest thing since Nutella on celery. Most of them are just here in hopes of becoming famous."

I fidget in my seat as Meredith drones on with advice, warnings, and the basics of the game, still trying to wrap my head around becoming the first girl on *Matchmaker*. It sounds like a rehash of a thousand other 'relationship' shows, but they've got some cool twists that make it seem a bit game-show, like a spinning wheel of potential dates and pressing the button to choose a guy. There's something about cards with pictures of the guys and me on them, but I'm too nervous to listen to

Meredith go over the details. I'm still so much in culture shock that I guess I'll just have to roll with it as it happens.

I still can't believe they chose me. I know there were thousands of women who sent in videos that were probably far sexier than mine. But Meredith told me it was my personality and girl next door beauty that so endeared me with the producers. Apparently, when they saw me talking and just being myself, they decided that they *had* to have me.

It's been an ego boost that they chose me, but while I feel a sense of pride, I can't help but feel the pressure. As the first Matchmaker, I feel like I'm going to have to be extraordinary. And I'm just . . . ordinary.

Just the thought of the pressure is making it difficult for me not to hurl my breakfast all over Meredith's Louboutin heels.

And then there's the tagline for the show. "Matchmaker . . . where you'll find your match and your happily ever after."

To me, it's almost eyeroll-worthy, but who knows? Maybe it'll catch on.

"You just said the guys are here for their own reasons," I interrupt as Meredith plays the credits music for me. "Am I supposed to become a great actor and fake it?"

Meredith makes a face, sort of like she wonders how I got through high school being this stupid. "Not necessarily. There might be a couple of genuine men here looking for love. It's your job to weed out the real from the douchebags, something I don't think you'll have a problem with. And if you do, that's what I'm here for—to help you choose and go down the right path. It might be a flawed process, but people do occasionally find real love on these shows. I've seen it with my own eyes." She pauses, looking reflective, and I wonder what her past is on this kind of show. "Now listen . . ."

She goes back to explaining the rules, but I get lost in my thoughts. Does anyone really find love on a TV show? I mean, I love watching them myself, but I'm not stupid. I don't expect them to live out their lives together after the show. Hell, the tabloids usually start popping up about couples splitting shortly after the show ends. Even if they do get married, it's only a countdown until the inevitable divorce.

Still, I can't deny that I'm feeling somewhat excited under all the anxiety. Even if I'm probably not going to find true love, getting to go out with a bunch of hot guys and do crazy, adventurous things sounds fun to me! Who knows, maybe one will be worth dating afterward. What single girl wouldn't be onboard with that?

Meredith is still going on about details of the show that I really should be paying close attention to when I hear footsteps and clicking heels behind me, followed by voices.

"Don't you even try it, biatch," a sassy, high-pitched male voice hisses. "I'm doing her makeup first."

A woman's sultry laugh follows. "Go ahead, sweetie. I'll try my best to keep her foundation pristine when I wash her hair."

"Bitch, please. You fuck up my makeup and I'll fuck up your life."

Standing in front of me, Meredith stops talking and shakes her head in disapproval at the newcomers, but I can't help but laugh. Curiosity forces me to turn my head to get a look at the pair.

A curvy woman with pink hair done in pinup curls and a petticoat peeking out of her circle dress approaches me, a smile on her face as she looks me up and down. "Hey, sweetie," she says, flashing a smile that I'm not sure is genuine. "I'm McKayla Quinn."

"Nice to meet you, McKayla," I begin to say, "I'm—"

She talks right over me, waving her hand. "You can call me Buffy. It's what everyone calls me anyway. I'll be your hairstylist for this shindig. But do me a favor. After I've spent hours making your hair perfect, keep it that way and we'll get along quite well. Hmm?" She finishes with a big open-mouth wink.

I smile politely. "I'll try my best—"

"And this is Brangelina Cooper," McKayla says over me again, gesturing at the flamboyantly dressed man beside her. He's tall and thin, wearing a pink shirt and designer blue jeans, his hair dyed platinum blonde with pink streaks. I think he has the bluest set of eyes I've ever seen and dimples that make me jealous. I wish mine were *half* as cute.

"His real name is Brad," McKayla continues, not even pausing to take a breath, "but he likes to be called Brangelina for some reason."

Brad scoffs. "Bitch, that's because I embody Angelina's beauty and Brad's hotness. And I've got a better ass than both."

"Apparently, no one's told him that Brad and Angie are finished," McKayla mutters. "And his ass isn't *that* good."

It's difficult to hide my smile as Brad offers me his hand and I take it.

"Excuse her," Brad says, smirking at McKayla. "She doesn't get out much. I'm delighted to inform you that I'll be your makeup artist while you're here." He leans in close and I catch a whiff of a woodsy feminine fragrance. "Between the two of us, we'll keep you primed and polished for your every close-up! I'll have your face looking beat and snatched at all times." He boasts as he flicks his wrist and snaps his fingers.

"Any questions before I take off?" Meredith asks, drawing my eyes back over to her. Judging from her body language, she isn't pleased at the interruption but she doesn't outright say anything. The look on her face alone says it all.

I have a million and one questions running through my mind, but I'm too tongue-tied to ask any of them. Plus, I don't want her to know that I was only half listening to her sermon. Instead, I slowly shake my head. "No, none right now."

"Good. I'll leave you in the dynamic duo's capable hands before we parade you in front of the producers." Meredith's expression doesn't match her complimentary words as she looks at the two like they're children. "They want to see how you'll look on camera all dolled up."

"Don't worry, Miss Mere," McKayla says in a way that makes Meredith grit her teeth, "We'll take good care of her."

"We promise," Brad echoes. "She'll look better than any fifty-dollar Sunset hooker by the time we're done."

Meredith lets out a dramatic sigh, raising her head to the ceiling. "Lord, if you two weren't so good at what you do, I'd . . ." she trails off, not finishing the threat.

"I don't care what you do with us as long as you pay me," McKayla says distractedly, turning her eyes on my hair. It looks like she's already making plans on the styles she wants to use.

"I know that's right," Brad echoes. "A bitch gotta eat. Those happy meals are expensive."

"Okay, I'll leave you to it," Meredith growls, throwing her hands up and walking to the doorway. Before she walks out, she stops to order curtly, "Just as long as you get her ready."

McKayla and Brad burst into laughter when she leaves. "I bet you her Spanx just got a little tighter, so tight she's about to burst out of it," Brad says.

McKayla laughs. "She did look a little flustered."

"Are you two always like this?" I'm forced to ask, shaking my head and giggling.

Brad looks at me like I'm crazy, doing a neck roll that I'm surprised doesn't make his head pop off. "Are you serious? Girl, yes! It's the only way we can do our job without dying of boredom. Not only will we get you camera-ready, but you'll be loosened up and ready to kick ass."

McKayla looks at me, gesturing toward the door. "All right, let's get a move on. Come on, baby girl, we gotta get you ready before Cruella Deville has our tits for breakfast."

Chuckling, I climb out of my seat and follow them several rooms over to what looks like a dressing room. Despite the constant back and forth, I like these two. Something tells me that they'll be the breath of fresh air that I need.

Brad has me change into a pair of comfy shorts and a

matching tank, explaining that I'll be able to take them off for wardrobe without messing up their masterpiece. I've definitely never been called that before. I sit in the salon-style chair and try not to flinch as they swarm around me. Sparring and gossiping at the same time, McKayla and Brad go about getting me ready.

I never knew I needed so much work to look presentable, and I have to wonder what the producers really thought when they saw me for the first time. I get shaved, plucked, exfoliated, washed, dried, straightened, and curled, and then it feels like Brad paints three pounds of makeup on my face. "Why not use a power sprayer next time?"

Brad laughs. "Don't tempt me. Now chin up!"

When they're done, they stand back, appraising their work. I stare at myself in the mirror in awe, hardly recognizing the girl looking back at me. Big hair, big makeup, big change. I look so different, I'm not sure if I should be shouting for joy or crying.

McKayla, on the other hand, isn't so impressed. "Why'd you pick that highlight?" she complains to Brad, peering at my face critically. "It's too glittery. She looks like a Vegas showgirl."

Brad twirls on McKayla like he's about to pop her. "Girl, are you nuts? You're looking at pure perfection right here!" he brags. He snaps his fingers, twirling his hips and sticking his bony ass out. "Honey, she's glowing like an angel dusted her cheeks." He looks at my hair, clucking his tongue. "Trying to talk bad about me, but what the hell is up with this Texas-sized bouffant on her head, huh? You could hide a family of rats up in there. Looks like a Tammy Faye bobble head!"

McKayla brandishes her curling iron in Brad's face. "Bitch, now you've gone too far. Those big, juicy curls will bounce every time she moves." She flips one of my curls and it bounces up and down for full effect. "You're just jealous because you only wish your ass had this much bounce."

Wow. I literally can't with these two, and I don't know if I should burst out laughing or cry. As they insult each other as if I'm not even there, my head ping-pongs between them, trying to decide which one is going to throw the first punch.

"I think you both did a good job," I finally say, silencing them. They both pause, looking at me. "I love the makeup and the hair." I'm not really sure if I love either, but if it will shut them up, I'll live with both.

"See, I told you she liked my angel cheeks," Brad boasts to McKayla, who rolls her eyes. "Jealous ho."

"Difference is, I don't need her opinion. I know my shit looks good."

They square off toward each other, hips popped and bitch faces in full effect. At this point, I'm convinced blows are about to rain, or maybe an epic bitch-slap fight with nails and glitter exploding everywhere. Before either can ask me to hold their earrings, I start to slink away from my chair in a desperate bid to get some distance from the inevitable battle. Keeping an eye on their staredown battle, I see the switch in Brad a moment before he bursts out laughing. And just like that, the tension is gone as the two laugh at each other and do a little high-five, causing me to let out a relieved sigh.

McKayla snaps her fingers at me when they're done. "All right, chickadee, let's get you to wardrobe. Our work here is done. You look good, and you should be loose enough to deal with getting poked and prodded."

I can't help but let out an audible groan.

McKayla chuckles at my distress. "What? You don't feel like Cinder-fucking-rella yet? Just look on the bright side. You'll get to try on more clothes than you've ever dreamed of."

Without another word, we're hustling down the hallways.

CHAPTER 4

HAYDEN

The hum of my Harley dies down as I slowly pull to a stop at the huge gate. I stare through the bars for a moment, spotting the looming mansion and beautiful manicured grounds. I don't know what the fuck Jay's gotten me into, but I hope it'll be worth the trouble.

I lean forward and press a button on the callbox attached to a brick column near the gate. Shit, even that's fancy. There's no static at all, nothing but smooth silence before a voice answers, asking for my identity.

"Hayden Bishop."

There's no reply, but the gate sweeps open and I slowly pull up toward the house.

A young guy who looks like he's only eighteen but is probably a bit older runs up and stops me. He's clutching a clipboard in his hands, looking rushed. "Name?"

"Hayden," I reply. "Hayden Bishop."

He looks down at his clipboard and then marks me off the

list, gesturing off to the side. "Park your bike over there." The guy begins to turn away and then stops. "Oh, and make sure that when you head inside, turn left down the first hall, and then go into the den on the right."

"Will do. Thanks." I quickly park my bike away from the circular driveway and make my way inside. Opulence greets me as I step through the door. This place is one of those homes that is best described as 'palatial', but that only scratches the surface. I've done a shoot or two in places like this, but as I'm walking down the hall, I feel my heart thump in my chest.

Walking toward me are a curvy pink-haired pinup and a flamboyant blond man. But that's not what's caught my eye. It's the gorgeous woman with full hair and makeup walking between them, her hips swaying with an unconscious seductiveness that bypasses all the layers of makeup that have been put on her. She's all dolled up, but for some reason, she only has on a simple tank top and shorts. I can hardly take my eyes off her beautiful face to notice. She's so stunning that it doesn't matter what she's wearing.

As they pass, she glances up and gives me the most perfectly sexy shy smile I've ever seen and my jaw drops. Jesus, what the fuck's wrong with me? The last time a girl tripped me up that easily, I was a hormonal high school boy who didn't know my dick from my emotions.

Fuck, looking at her gorgeous smile, I can't help it. I have to say something. Before I can speak, the man motions me sharply down the hallway.

"Uh-uh, honeybuns. You gotta wait your turn for Miss Thing here, I don't care how hot you are. Now move along!"

Obviously dismissed, I watch as they continue down the hall

away from me, the gay guy swishing his hips as if he's in competition with the two women next to him. I'm forced to laugh a little at the ridiculousness of it all. Shaking my head, I smile. Hopefully, I'll see Miss Thing again if I don't get sent home immediately. Maybe this trip will be worth it, after all.

As soon as I step through the door to the den, the smell of cologne assaults my nostrils. Lots of it, to the point that I want to either gag or sneeze. The room must be filled with at least forty other dudes, all seated in chairs, waiting. They're all primped, dressed in their best, and dandied up to the point that it's nearly eye-rolling for some of them. I'm going to stick out like a sore thumb, but maybe that's a good thing.

With so many here, it's not a sight that I welcome. It means more competition for me in some form or another, but I'm used to it. I figure this is going to be just like any other cattle call I've been on. I just need to make the most of it and do my best.

I find a chair and settle in to wait my turn as the men around me chatter, a lot of them boasting about their accomplishments. After listening for a bit, I engage in the small talk, wanting to find out who my competition is. I'm sure most of them are just here for the opportunity of being on TV. But the more I talk, I'm surprised that there's a few other than me who don't seem to be braggarts looking for a quick fifteen minutes of fame.

It's not long before we're getting called to the back, one by one. I sit patiently as each name is called out, watching the reactions of the men who come out. Some of them come out after a few minutes and sit down with smiles on their faces, while others come out with grim expressions and leave without saying a word.

After what seems like an eternity, my name is finally called.

"Hayden Bishop."

I get up from my seat and walk into the adjourning office. Inside, there's an impeccably dressed woman who reminds me of Meryl Streep standing before a table that seats a group of men and women. They must be the producers or other execs.

The woman's face lights up when she sees me, and she gives me a warm smile. "Hello, Hayden," she greets me. "It's nice to meet you. I'm Meredith Ward, executive producer of the show." She gestures to her side. "And these are my wonderful colleagues."

I nod at everyone. "It's a pleasure to meet you all."

Meredith grins. "That it is. Shall we get right to it?"

"Of course."

Meredith starts by asking stuff she should already know based on my resume, but I answer each question with a confident smile. I make sure to flash the dimples Jay said would be my ticket in the door. I don't usually use them intentionally, but whatever. If it works, it works.

"And how is your modeling coming along?" Meredith asks. "I understand you're in high demand."

I don't bother to correct her about my popularity. It must be something Jay added to my profile. "I just finished a shoot before coming here, actually. It ended up being a little more full-throttle than what I was expecting, honestly."

Meredith and the other executives laugh and I grin. After, she grows quiet and I feel a little twinge of anxiety returning as she looks to her colleagues. They don't say anything but their faces are expressive.

After another moment, Meredith walks over and picks up a piece of paper off the desk and hands it over to me, along with a pen. "All right, Hayden," she announces with a smile. "I think you are what we're looking for. Please sign the NDA and we'll get down to the details."

A sense of relief washes over me as I take the paper. Excited to find out what the big secret is, I hastily sign. Besides, this is just a standard one-page NDA. It's not like I'm signing my life over.

Meredith smiles in approval as she takes it back and slides it over to one of her colleagues. Then she picks up another form, this one multiple pages. She fingers it with one manicured nail as she speaks. "So in case you're wondering, you're here for a show called Matchmaker."

She explains about how it's a new game show-meets-love connection-type reality show and that I would be one of many male suitors. Hearing it, I frown. I definitely wasn't expecting something like this. I've always thought these shows about finding love on TV were pretty much bullshit.

If I do this, I can only picture the shit my parents will get back home. Dad will probably laugh his ass off at me, and Mom will talk about how tactless it is.

Meredith appears to notice the distaste on my face. "Think about it. You do well here and you'd have a name in the industry. You won't be kissing up to pervy photogs or scrabbling at cattle calls for runway work." She grins. "Just think of it as a platform to promote yourself. A form of free advertisement."

I feel the weight of all eyes in the room on me and I scratch the back of my neck. Shit, I'm being put on the fucking spot. The only thing that sounds fun about this right now are the adventures. When else am I going to get to travel for free? When I don't reply right away, Meredith speaks up. "Don't you want to at least see her?"

Taken out of my reverie, I focus my eyes on Meredith's face. "Huh? Her?" I ask in confusion.

Meredith smirks. "The lovely lady you'll be competing over."

She doesn't give me a chance to respond, walking over and grabbing a glossy piece of paper from the end of the table and handing it to me.

My heart jumps as my eyes fall on the same face of the girl I saw in the hallway. The hair isn't the same and she doesn't have on the gallons of makeup, but it's definitely her. I'm slack-jawed as I stare at the photo, transfixed by her beauty. She looks even more gorgeous without all the face paint.

"Hayden?" Meredith asks when the silence stretches on for far too long. She's looking at me with a confident grin like she knows what my answer will be.

I can't believe I'm doing this . . . but fuck it. I don't have anything else going on anyway. I'm in.

I swallow the lump in my throat and stare at the papers in Meredith's hands. "Where do I sign?"

CHAPTER 5

EMILY

"*G*od, I'm so nervous!" I hiss.

I grip the fabric of the blue cocktail dress the producers chose for me, my heart beating a mile a minute as I try to calm myself. I'm totally freaking out right now, somewhere between overwhelmed and excited and maybe about to puke. After two days of weirdness as I'm made "familiar" with the mansion via highly regulated escort, today's the day we officially start filming. The reality of my situation has suddenly become all too real. I'm excited, but butterflies are still swarming in my belly.

"Chill, chica," Brad whispers to me as he sees my right foot nervously tap-dancing to its own tune. We're standing with McKayla in a prop room that's going to later serve as the cocktail room for my suitors, waiting for filming to start. There's a hubbub of activity going on, the production crew running to and fro, moving props and shouting orders. For the past half hour, I've watched the commotion and done nothing but fret over all the little things that could go wrong.

Brad notices and pats me on the back. "Everything is going to be fine. You look absolutely stunning."

The whole day, McKayla and Brad have tried their best to calm me down. As they did my hair and makeup, Brad was even joking about the bright red lips he gave me.

"Girl, I do believe I've given you the world's best set of blowjob lips!" he quipped, snapping his fingers at my fierce look. "It's going to drive all those dicks out there crazy!"

Sure, it worked, and I laughed, but it only took away my worries for a moment. And I couldn't help but hope that the guys I meet tonight aren't thinking that about my lips because then that'll mean I'm sending the wrong message. I'm not a slut. And sending the wrong message is the last thing I want to do on TV.

And what do I know about being on camera anyway? I'll probably fudge up the whole thing.

McKayla and Brad have assured me there's nothing to filming since I don't have actual lines and that I should just be myself. After all, that's why they chose me, apparently. So far, that hasn't helped. I think what's driving me crazy the most is meeting all of these men and being expected to have chemistry with several of them, something I know isn't possible.

And how am I supposed to know who is genuine and who is not?

No one cares if the love on the show is real. All that matters is whether it appears that way, says a small voice in the back of my mind. *It's the fantasy of perfect love. Not the truth.*

I don't know why the thought bothers me. I love to watch these shows and I can't get enough of them. But now I'm on the other side.

"That's easy for you to say," I reply to Brad, tearing my eyes away from a camera man carrying his equipment balanced on his shoulder as he rushes across the room. "You're not the one who has to go out there and be tossed in front of a pack of wolves."

Brad lets out a snort and gives me a little shimmy. "Girl, please, I wish I was in your shoes. I'd yell for them to bring it on. They could eat all of this good stuff," he says as he gestures to encompass his whole body.

"Except they'd probably get sick from eating tainted meat," McKayla butts in. "And then filming would be a wrap."

"Ain't nothing tainted here, sweetheart," Brad gloats, doing a little twirl as he pops his ass twice. "All of this tootsie roll is sweet. Sweet enough to eat."

McKayla laughs and shakes her head and then looks at me with sympathy. "I'm sorry if we're not helping, chica, but like Brad said, you'll be fine."

I shake my head. "Hearing you two is actually helping. It's keeping my mind occupied."

McKayla smiles at me. "Darlin', if I looked like you look right now, all I would be worried about is how many hearts I'm going to break tonight when all the men see me."

Warmth flows through my chest at her compliment. Even I have to admit that I look good, thanks to McKayla and Brad. My hair is done up into a spectacular updo with wisps of hair that cascade around my face. Despite Brad's comment about my lips, he's gifted me with a fierce face mask that channels a bit of catwalk. The cocktail dress is hugging my curves in all the right places, topped off with a sparkling diamond necklace and three-inch black heels that I can barely walk in.

"Thank you," I reply softly, blushing.

Meredith sweeps into the room like a tornado before McKayla can reply, shouting orders and making demands. As usual, she's dressed sharp as a tack in a black jumpsuit and matching black pumps, a white belt wrapped around her waist and not a hair on her head out of place.

The flurry of activity increases at Meredith's commands, and the production crew goes into overdrive bringing the set to life. At the moment, I'm struck by how fake the setup is, but my frazzled nerves keep me from dwelling on it.

"Hey!" Meredith yells at a poor young stagehand carrying a vase that looks too large for him, gesturing wildly, "Watch where you're going with that thing! It cost the studio a fortune." She looks like she's about to scold him further when her eyes fall on me and she forgets about him as she walks over.

"Well, don't you look beautiful," Meredith says, stopping in front of me and pursing her lips as she looks me up and down. "I knew we made the right choice. All you have to do is deliver on bringing the drama."

I go pale, feeling sick to my stomach at her words. It's a cold reminder of how the entire show is riding on my shoulders. Drama? I'm boring. I'm anything *but* drama.

Before I can reply, Brad clears his throat.

Meredith snorts. "If you're looking for a compliment for doing a job that the studio pays you good money for, then you'll be waiting until you're old and gray."

Brad goes silent, but I'm almost certain I hear him mutter under his breath, "Good money, my flat ass."

Meredith ignores him and for the first time, her face softens as she reaches out and places a hand on my shoulder. "How are you feeling, doll?"

I part my lips to lie, but I think better of it. "Just a bit nervous is all. I don't want to screw anything up."

"Oh, honey, you can't worry yourself about that," Meredith tells me. "You'll do fine. We picked you out of thousands of applicants, and we're usually a good judge of character. If all fails, just picture them naked and giggle all the time. You'll come off as cute and endearing to the audience, if not a little ditzy." She gestures at the room's exit. "But if you'll just follow me, we need to get you in position for the men's arrival."

I feel like a knock-kneed duck as I follow Meredith across the room and out to the manicured grounds, nearly stumbling as my heels sink into the grass. Brad and McKayla follow under the guise of making sure my hair and makeup stay on point, but I think they're mostly lending me some much-needed moral support.

The sun is just setting as we make it out, basking the mansion in its orange glow. In spite of the setup, I'm in total awe of the gorgeous scene in front of me, taking a moment to memorize the sight before we begin. From what I've been able to gather, the ceremony starts at dusk, any minute now.

"Here," Meredith says, stopping at an erected three-step dais before the roundabout driveway. She gives me her hand to help me up the steps and I turn around to face her.

"There," she says, beaming. "You look perfect. Oh, and we

can't forget this." She takes a tiny wireless mic from Nate, who hovers nearby, silently anticipating Meredith's need. Attaching the mic to the front of my dress and the sound pack on my back, she surveys me one more time. Turning to McKayla and Brad, she says, "I do have to hand it to you guys. For all of your crazy cattiness, she looks great."

McKayla and Brad look shocked at the compliment, but she doesn't give them a chance to reply. "Okay, I have to go make sure the set is coming along inside. Emily, hold your mark for the ceremony. Joe, the cameraman, will be out here when it's time to start filming." She points at McKayla and Brad. "You two can stay out here for support, but only interrupt if Emily needs her hair or makeup fixed."

"*Ja wohl, Fraulein!*" Brad says with a mock salute.

Meredith ignores him and gives me a wink as she walks off.

I'm standing on the dais, shaking like a leaf as studio crews rush outside to set up lighting and put large vases filled with roses around me. Despite the pep talk from Meredith, my anxiety seems to have only gotten worse, my heart pounding in my chest like a war drum as the flurry of activity around me begins to make me dizzy.

McKayla is the first to notice that I look like I'm about to have a panic attack. She climbs up on the dais and begins fluffing my hair. "Breathe, chickadee, breathe," she whispers in my ear so the nearby crew doesn't hear. "Brad and I have your back. And you look fucking hot! You have nothing to worry about. You're going to knock them off their feet. Just chill, smile, and have fun."

She pats me on my back, and for the first time tonight, I feel some of my anxiety ebbing and my confidence returning.

I can do this, I chant to myself. *Just be myself, but more confident and more chill.*

And how many reality shows have I watched anyway? I'm practically a fucking expert. There's no reason for me to be scared. Lord knows, I've seen enough episodes to know how this will roll, even if this is my first time participating in one.

The greeting ceremony should be a piece of cake. Each guy is supposed to walk up and introduce himself. Then after everyone has their moment, we'll all mingle and chat it up to get to know each other.

Apparently, cameras and mics are hidden all over the place to catch all conversation, even whispered ones.

"All right, everyone, ready?" Meredith yells, reappearing on the edge of the set with a walkie talkie in her hand. She motions for Brad and McKayla to scram. "They'll arrive any moment."

"Good luck, chica," McKayla whispers, jumping off the dais.

"You've got this," Brad echoes as the two head off to the side and the cameraman gets in place.

"Cue the limos!" yells Meredith.

A black SUV limo pulls up the driveway. I have to remember to take a breath as it rolls to a stop a few feet from me and put a smile on my face. There's a long pause as the suited driver walks around to stand by the door, and I swear they can hear my heart pounding on the mic.

The door opens and my breath catches in my throat.

A tall blond man in a tux steps out of the limo. It feels like I've seen him before, and he walks up with a swagger that just won't quit.

"Hello, Emily," he says in his deep voice, stopping right in front of me. Up close, I can smell his cologne. Spicy, masculine, but not too strong. His dirty blond hair is slicked to the side, and his chiseled jawline and perfect white smile are making me weak in the knees, his piercing blue eyes cutting straight through me. "You look absolutely beautiful."

For a moment, I'm at a loss for words.

Respond, you idiot!

"T–Thank you," I say, smiling. "You don't look so bad yourself . . .?" I look pointedly at him, raising an eyebrow.

"Hayden," he says in a voice that makes me want to melt. "Hayden Bishop. I'm excited to get to know you. I have a feeling we're going to be a match."

"We'll see about that," I say lightheartedly. "There might be more of you where you came from," I add as I cut my eyes to the SUV before locking eyes with him again.

"Nope. There's only one me. I'm all you could ever need . . . or handle."

My face turns scarlet. He's got confidence. I like it. Before I can say anything, Meredith yells, "Next!"

Hayden looks disappointed, like he wants to say more, but he pulls me in for a friendly embrace. I'm enveloped by the heat radiating from his body, and I'm disappointed when he lets go of me and heads inside.

I let out a sigh, trying to release some tension and wishing I had a fan. That wasn't so bad. If they're all like him, shit, I'm in for a treat.

Next out is another handsome gentleman, a clean-shaven, dark brunette with hazel eyes. Like Hayden, he's dressed in a dapper tux and has looks that could kill. But I don't feel quite the same connection.

"If they'd have told me you were this beautiful, I would've dressed up," the guy says in a voice that has a slight silky rasp to it.

I have to giggle at his compliment. "Thank you."

"I'm Lee," he says, taking my hand and brushing his lips across it. He knows just how to do it, and I feel goose-bumps rising on my flesh. "Lee Dixon. I'm excited to get to know you and see if we're a match," he says, saying almost the same thing as Hayden. I have a feeling they've been coached to say those words somewhere in their intro-duction.

"Nice to meet you, Lee," I say politely, flashing him a dazzling smile as he lets go of my hand. "It's a pleasure meeting you."

Meredith calls next, and in moments, Lee is gone and guy after guy climbs out of the limos to greet me. Some take my hand and some give light hugs. Some are casual and some are intense.

But they do have one thing in common. Each one seems just as handsome as the last, and it gets hard not to mix up names with faces. Something tells me I'm going to need cue cards to keep up with them all, but one good thing is that I find myself relaxing with each encounter.

By the time the entire cast has their turn greeting me and have headed inside, I feel dizzy but grateful that the cere-mony is over. Meredith walks over with a smile on her face as I step down from the dais.

"How'd I do?" I ask, feeling a bit of uncertainty return.

"Wonderful," she replies, filling me with relief. "Plenty of good footage, and you came off well."

Off to the side, Brad and McKayla give me thumbs up. "You rocked it, girl!"

Meredith glances at them, then looks back at me. "All right, Emily, time to head inside for the cocktail scene. I need you to mingle around with the guys, feel them out a little. And remember, always act like you're having a good time. If you have to chew a guy out on the first night, make it good. I wanna see his balls hanging from your bed stand, got it?"

She walks off, leaving me alone in my thoughts. It takes only moments for my anxiety to return. How the hell am I supposed to choose? Better yet, how do I know who's genuine and who's fake? Because to me, all of them were pretty fucking convincing so far.

As I make my way into the mansion and try to still my beating heart, I realize this is going to be a long night. I need to take my blinders off and get ready to spot the snakes. Because despite all the charming smiles and the honey-tongued compliments, I know they're there, just waiting to strike.

The funny thing is, out of thirty guys, I can't remember a single name and attach it with a face. Except one.

Hayden.

CHAPTER 6

HAYDEN

I sit back and watch Emily making her way from group to group in the lounge room, my eyes glued to her like a hawk. She looks like Venus embodied in an updated wardrobe in that blue dress. The damn thing is hugging her body in all the right places, and I'm having a hard time keeping my desire in check.

I still can't get over how she looked on that dais when I pulled up. Standing there in that dress, a perfect blend of wide-eyed innocent and girl-next-door siren, she was amazing. And from the first words out of her mouth, I knew that I'm in it to win it. My blood heats just thinking about her and all the ways I can corrupt her, make her sweet little body beg for mine. I'm forced to adjust my collar as I swallow, letting the fantasy visions go for now to focus as she moves around the room.

She's doing a great job of chatting with the guys, trying to be sociable and pretending to have a good time, but I can see her nervousness. Every once in awhile, she twirls a lock of hair around a finger and giggles. But her laughter doesn't ring true to me. It seems forced.

She's probably bored to tears by the same questions over and over. Her voice is starting to get monotonous and her eyes are starting to look glossy. Not all of the men are badgering her with questions. A few of them go straight to bragging about how amazing they are, thinking she'll be impressed.

I have to laugh at how ridiculous they sound. Total douchebags, going on and on about their cars, their jobs, and their bank accounts. If every guy in here were like that, they'd have to wrap the show because Emily would be mine before the clock struck twelve.

Unfortunately, I do see some actual contenders, seemingly normal guys just like me who carry an air of authenticity about them. I recognize one of them, a Daniel Garza whom I shared a limo with.

I shift in my seat when I hear Emily approach the group of men next to me. My lips curl in distaste when I recognize Lee Dixon. He was also in the same limo as me. He, more than anyone else, makes my stomach churn. He sets his wine glass aside and jumps to his feet to take her hand, bringing it to his lips for a kiss that lasts too long for my liking.

"Nice to see you again, Emily," Lee says with aplomb that makes me grit my teeth. The dude is acting like the consummate gentleman when he was the complete opposite in the limo. Something about how he'd spent last night dreaming of choking her with his cock. I have to make sure she stays far away from this asshole. "I'm honored to be one of your suitors. And I have to tell you that you grow more stunning by the minute in that dress." As he says the last part, he uses her hand to turn her around in a little twirl, his eyes roving down her body.

Emily looks flustered by it all, and judging by the blush on her cheeks, she's feeling him. I smother the surge of envy that swells from the depth of my stomach at the smile on her face. Even though I don't like Lee, I can't let him or anyone else make me lose control over my emotions. I'm here to play a game just like everyone else, and I won't win by getting worked up the moment someone is trying to mack on Emily.

Keeping a level head, I watch their interaction, and I have to admit, Lee's smooth and talks a good game despite his ugliness in the limo. The other poor schmucks in that group have barely spoken to Emily at all. It's almost like Lee's entranced her into a private conversation in the middle of the party.

I start to get irritated when their conversation goes on longer than it should, but thankfully, Meredith puts an end to it. She's been watching on the sidelines. "Cut! Emily, move to the next group, please."

"Yes, Ma'am," I hear Emily mutter. She gives Lee a little wink, laughing at some joke he whispers to her before she approaches my group.

Her eyes immediately fall on me and she freezes, her lips parting in surprise and a blush that rivals the one she had for Lee popping up on her cheeks.

I jump to my feet, getting to her before anyone in the group can. I know I have to be imposing, towering over her at 6'3" when she seems to be no more than 5'4", but I peg her for loving tall men. "Hello again, Emily," I say to her. Her perfume is entrancing, a woodsy fragrance that makes my head spin. "Having a good time so far?"

For a moment, Emily doesn't reply, her mouth opening and closing before she manages a smile. "I am," she says, blushing slightly. God, I love the sound of her voice. Sweet and pure, yet a note of sultriness buried underneath. She's got a wholesome vibe, but I can tell there's another side to her ready to burst out at any moment, and damned if I don't want to be the man who unleashes her. "I'm just having a hard time remembering everyone's name." She giggles, almost in a way that makes me feel like she's been told to laugh just for appearance's sake. "I may end up needing cue cards or something."

I chuckle. "Do you remember mine?" I feel like there's no way she could forget mine, but I brace myself for her to say no anyway. After all, there were twenty-nine guys after me.

"Of course," she says softly, surprising me as she looks up at me. "Hayden Bishop."

Warmth fills my stomach. She even remembered my last name. That's a good sign. "Oh, the full name too. I must have left a good impression then," I say, grinning.

"You did," she says softly. Our eyes lock, and it feels like an invisible current flows between us. She seems to sense it because she dips her chin, smiling shyly as she reaches for the lock of her hair.

I intercept her hand, gently lowering it, and then push the curl behind her ear myself. "No need to be nervous," I tell her. "We're all just trying to get to know you. And for good reason."

She bites her lip as she nods, and all I can think is that I wish I could bite that lip myself. "I know, and I want to get to know you—all of you."

I'm the only one you need to know, I want to tell her. *The rest don't matter.*

"So, what brings you to the show?" Emily asks. "Are you really looking to find your perfect match?"

I open my lips to reply, but Meredith interrupts. "Emily, move it along."

Emily looks at me apologetically and I feel sorry for her. There's no way she could get to know a guy in less than an hour, let alone thirty men in that time.

"Sorry," she says simply. There's not much else to say.

"It's all right," I say. "We'll have plenty of time to get to know each other better."

She blushes at the confidence in my words as she moves away. My eyes never leave her face as she goes from group to group, making small chat. A couple of guys in my group keep up the conversation around us, but I barely notice them because I'm so focused on Emily. Looking at her body language, I try to get more of a read on who my competition is.

After another twenty minutes, Meredith calls out, "All right, time for our first elimination scene. Guys, line up in the yard in front of the hedge backdrop. Emily, come over by the table."

We move where instructed and listen as Meredith explains that this initial cut is the biggest of the season, dropping our group from thirty to fifteen in one night. There's a few grumbles from the guys about not wanting to go home so soon, but they knew this was coming. Besides, those who get cut still get to stay on the grounds until initial shooting wraps, so it's a free vacation either way.

Emily seems flustered about having to make such a large cut so quickly, but Meredith walks up to her, Nate at her side with his ever-present clipboard. I can't hear them, but I see Emily's eyes lighting on each guy and Nate making a corresponding mark as she goes down the line. A few times, I see Meredith talking to Emily about a suitor and it seems like Meredith gets her way with her choice of guys, Emily nodding along with her.

Finally, the scene is set and Emily is shepherded to stand in front of the line of guys. Nate hands each of us card with a split image of our own headshots and Emily's, telling us to hold them face down.

Nate hands Emily a card, and Meredith yells, "Action!"

Emily recites some lines. "Hi, Matt. It's time to see if we have a match." And as they both turn their cards over, holding them up for the camera, I can see that the matching split image is shown on both cards.

The next fellow isn't so lucky, and when they turn their cards over, hers is blank. No match. He gives her a chaste kiss to the cheek and exits the scene, walking over the catering table.

As Emily works her way down the line, I realize some of these guys never had a chance. There just wasn't enough time, and they didn't seize the small opportunity they had. Reality TV just isn't for them. Hell, it isn't for me either. But seeing Emily, I *have* to win.

Thankfully, a few of the loudmouth guys get sent off too, one of whom doesn't take it too well. After recovering from his shock, the jackass goes straight to anger and starts loudly muttering about how the producers will hear from his agent. I wonder if they'll edit that out or leave it for dramatic effect.

Emily seems a little confused and wary, but she continues down the row.

She matches a couple more guys, including Lee. I have to admit, that match makes me grit my teeth, but there's nothing I can do about it. I knew the sly bastard wasn't getting cut tonight. He's got too much charisma and, at least in front of Emily, he's been a perfect gentleman. I'll just have to bide my time and expose him for the snake that he is.

And then it's my turn.

Standing in front of me, I realize she's shaking. God, I wish I could take her in my arms right here and now and tell her everything will be all right. But they've made it clear what the rules are, and that's out of bounds.

I am allowed to touch her, though, so I reach out and take her hand, covering it with my own. "It's okay, Emily. You can do this," I tell her in a reassuring voice.

There's a long pause as she stares up at me with wide, doe eyes. There's no way she's cutting me, but for a moment, my confidence wavers. Then, she suddenly smiles and recites her lines and we flip our cards over simultaneously.

It's a match.

CHAPTER 7

EMILY

"Oh, my God," I moan as I get ready to head down to hair and makeup. I haven't seen McKayla and Brad since last night and I can't believe I'm actually looking forward to their bickering. "That was one of the hardest, most awkward things I've ever had to do in my life!"

I'm no wallflower, but being the center of attention with all those guys felt *so* weird. All the grins, all the compliments, started to make me feel dizzy at one point, and I was grateful when Meredith called to cut.

I hated sending some of the men home, too. Some, I hardly even got to speak to. But I had little choice in the matter. When Meredith and Nate went through the list with me, they pressured me to keep those who were more 'camera friendly', so even though I wish I'd had more time to get to know four of the guys, I had to cut them. Instead, I kept the fifteen who most matched what I'm looking for, and what *Meredith's* looking for.

Luckily, after all the non-match guys had been escorted off

set, it was a little more celebratory. We all jumped around and cheered like we'd won the homecoming game.

Lee even picked me up, bouncing me like I'd scored the winning goal, although honestly, I think he might've just been feeling my ass. If he wasn't so hot, I might have more of a problem with it, because I don't normally move that fast. Besides, I'm hoping it was just for the cameras, so I'll give him a pass.

We'd shot one more scene last night, where Meredith had us all gather around a big lit-up wheel and I spun it to see what our date activity would be for today. That's how I found out our first group date is going to be bowling, and I haven't bowled since I was a kid with gutter guards. I can't imagine this will go well, but with the guys, I think it'll be fun.

I let out a sigh, feeling slightly depressed as I look at myself in the mirror.

"Wonder what they'd think if they saw me now?" I whisper, running my hands through my disheveled mane that looks wild from a night of tossing and turning. Without all the hair extensions, makeup, and false eyelashes, I look nothing at all like the diva who rocked the party last night.

I do love how I look all jazzed up, but a part of me thinks that it's a bad thing. Whomever I end up choosing is going to be so used to seeing me made up like a doll.

The thought depresses me, but I have shit to do. I push down my worries and leave the room, making my way to hair and makeup.

"Holy shit, girlfriend, what happened to you?" Brad exclaims in horror when I walk through the door. Unlike me, he and McKayla look fresh-faced, with Brad wearing neon pink pants and a white dress shirt while McKayla looks like she's channeling Dita von Teese for a night on the town in her painted-on low-cut mermaid dress, fishnets, and sky-high platform heels. Her hair is styled like Peg Bundy and I wonder just how much product it takes to poof it up like that. As I stare at her hair, Brad questions me. "Did you sleep with all fifteen guys last night . . . all at the same time?" He actually sounds a bit hopeful that maybe I did.

I give him a glare as I make my way over to the chair, trying not to giggle. "Oh, shut up!"

McKayla laughs, her hands on her hips. "You tell 'em, girl. Don't listen to him. He's just jealous, wishing he could get in that meat pile."

Brad looks at McKayla like she's lost her mind. "Whatever, bitch. I'll have you know that I've made more than a few straight men change teams. I already know three that I'd turn gay so fast that two-dollar weave you're wearing would fly off your head." He does his twirl and pops his hip, his signature move it seems. "No one can resist this booty." To reiterate the point, he gives his ass cheek a little smack.

I laugh as I climb in my chair and McKayla makes a face of disgust. "Bitch, please. I've seen better asses on a donkey."

"Oh, thank you!" I sigh, wiping at my eyes. It's only been a minute and I'm already feeling better. "I so needed that after last night. It was so stressful."

McKayla gives me a sympathetic look as she grabs a flat iron off the vanity. "It sure looked like it, but you need to relax. You've got a lot more to go."

There's a couple of moments of silence as she gets started. "Well?" McKayla asks me as she's messing with my hair.

"Well, what?" I ask.

"Spill it, chickadee. Who's your favorite?" she demands. Before I can reply, she adds, "It's Lee, isn't it? When I saw him twirl you, girl, I about swooned myself! I love a man who can dance, and that man looks like he's got some moves." McKayla's eyes are twinkling as she speaks, a look of infatuation on her face. Remembering Lee's smoothness, I can't blame her.

Brad doesn't share her opinion, shaking his head almost immediately as he uses the a wet wipe to remove any residual makeup from my face and then applies a primer. "Oh, hell, no. That one is a slick willy, and I don't mean that in the sense that he'll ease on in. I'd watch him with sharp eyes if I were you."

"I'm watching," I mutter. "Trust me, I'm watching." I pause for a moment as Brad starts applying foundation with his brush. "Is there anyone else I should watch out for?"

I watch Brad purse his lips in the mirror. "I think that Matt one is a cutie, but I don't think it's my ego talking when I say he might be more interested in me than you. Not sure what that means for you, Miss Em. But if you cut him, I'm making a trip over to the elimination house to see if my gaydar tingles are right . . . at least for the night."

I laugh at their antics as we go through the list of remaining suitors, discussing who might be here for real or who might be fake. While we chat, McKayla makes a point of telling me to keep my hands out of my hair and stop messing with her genius work.

"What about Hayden?" I ask as both Brad and McKayla draw close to being finished.

McKayla lets out a dreamy sigh as she finishes my hair and

gives it a satisfied pat. "That man is hot with a capital Fuck Me, Please. Between him and Lee, they just might burn this place to the ground."

"For once, I agree with the witch," Brad says, putting on his finishing touch, my long, fake lashes.

Warmth flows through my chest, grateful that both Brad and McKayla are people who are willing to talk straight with me. I know it's only been a few days, but they already feel like friends.

"Finished!" Brad announces as he appraises his work, prodding me out of my seat. "Tell me I'm not an artist!"

I have to blink rapidly before I can see, but when my vision clears enough to see my reflection in the mirror, I can't help myself, nodding. Once again, I look like a movie star thanks to them. I feel a surge of confidence seeing the change from how I looked just twenty minutes ago. "You do good work."

"Damn, girl, you're drop-dead gorgeous," McKayla says proudly, smiling at her hair job. "You look even better than last night."

I flush at her compliment. "Thank you."

Brad smacks me on my ass, causing me to jump in surprise. "All right, we did our part, now get out there and get a hole in one!

I laugh, correcting him. "Sorry, nasty boy, but we're bowling, not golfing."

With a smirk, Brad sasses back. "Oh, I wasn't talking about the game, darlin'!"

I shake my head as I walk out. I just can't with him, but I still manage to hear McKayla teasing, "Dumb ass, it's one in a hole, not a hole in one because she's the one with holes."

Brad smarts right back. "Bitch, girls ain't the only ones with holes. Trust me on that."

I'm still grinning when I walk to wardrobe. They quickly dress me in some Grease version of a bowling alley outfit, but I have to admit the black cigarette pants look painted on my curves, and the flirty tie of the shirt at my waist is flattering.

Feeling myself a bit, I follow Nate to the bowling alley. Yes, this mansion has a fucking bowling alley. Who lives like this? Certainly not me. The guys are sitting around at little cocktail tables and all eyes turn to me as I enter. It's not like any bowling alley I've ever seen, though. Everything is luxurious, and the only thing I'd recognize from a normal bowling alley is the ball return machine. At least, no bowling alley I've ever seen has leather padded benches to wait your turn on.

I swear, my heart pounds a mile a minute and I almost turn and run out of the room as anxiety grips me. You'd think I'd be used to this by now, but apparently not. There's one face my eyes fall on almost immediately, but I drag my eyes away as Hayden's eyes meet mine.

God, he looks even hotter than he did last night. His bowling shirt fits him like a glove, and the sparkle in his eye when he sees me is thrilling.

Meredith ushers me in, unaware of my anxiety, already ranting. "You're late. Hop on your mark." Then she turns and hollers louder to everyone else. "All right, people, take turns bowling and talk to each other. Needs to look like a big bowling party. Top two scores will be in the running for a solo date with Emily for lunch."

With a clap, she settles in to watch the monitors.

I shove down my anxiety and wave, putting on a bright, fresh smile. "Hi, guys. Who's ready to show me how to bowl?"

There are some smiles and laughs, and a few hands shoot up in the air.

"Anyone good at this?" I ask. "I haven't bowled since I was a kid, so go easy on me."

Somewhere in the back, I hear a deep voice. "I never go easy on my dates. They take it the way I give it or not at all."

It sounds like Mark, and I see Luke laughing a bit as he nudges him and nods his head like it was a good joke.

Uh, yeah . . . asshole alert.

It's one thing for a guy to boss me in the heat of the moment but a whole other thing to be frat boy, locker room mouthing about it in front of everyone. On fucking camera.

Pretending not to be annoyed, I beam at the men as if I'm so excited to be here. "Let's get started, shall we?"

The staff's already set up the computers, so all we have to do is have me push the big green button on the console to start everything. I do okay, knocking down a few pins in my first two frames. A couple of the men are actually really good, and some hit gutter balls every time, but most are somewhere in the middle.

One of them, Shawn, is getting visibly frustrated at his continued lack of success and seems to be on the edge of a temper tantrum. Seeing his behavior really turns me off and ruins the mood. If he can't control his temper for something like this, how mad would he get at something actually important?

Nope. He's gone as soon as I get the chance. As the game continues, I find myself surprised at how I'm actually getting into this, watching the guys and being analytical about their behavior, what appeals to me and what doesn't. And whom I'd like to keep around for a while longer to find out more about.

I know some, Meredith included, may not like my choices, but at the end of the day, there can only be one final Match. So hopefully, there are no hard feelings. My next time up, Hayden approaches with a smile that makes me weak in the knees. I smile back as he speaks, not letting him on to how attracted I am to him.

"Hey, Emily," he says in that sultry voice that can melt chocolate, "Can I show you something?" He points at my hands. "Not hating on your skills, but I noticed that you turn your wrist as you let go of the ball. That's why it keeps going left, and you could really hurt your wrist. Do you mind?" He's gesturing toward me and I realize he's going to show me. I smile and nod. He steps behind me, nestling my ass in his crotch as he puts his left hand on my hip. He wraps his right hand around my wrist, holding it straight as he leads my arm back and forth a few times, making sure I get the feel of the move.

My cheeks burn scarlet at the proximity of his body and my temperature rises a few degrees. Fuck, I'm feeling something, all right, but I'm not sure it's my bowling skills improving.

He steps away, our eyes meeting, and he gives me another heated smile. It's contagious, and I smile back, wanting to yell for someone to bring me a damn fan!

Considering the setup, Hayden could've played that much dirtier, but he seems like a gentleman and I appreciate that.

Taking his advice, I consciously swing my arm back and forth, letting go and watching with delight as the ball rolls straight down the alley and slowly knocks every pin down.

"Woo-hoo!" I scream joyfully, clapping for myself. I jump up and down, turning to give Hayden a hug. "Thanks! You were right!"

Hayden hugs me back for a moment, then releases me, raising his hand for a high-five. From there on, we continue bowling, and after the tenth frame, Lee and Hayden are the top two. I'm not really surprised. They both seem eager to win and are pushing each other to the max.

I clap my hands together and smile as if they're all my Prince Charmings and I'm their princess. "That was a lot of fun today, guys! Thanks for mostly being good sports and making this fun." I pause, taking a deep breath and drawing out the moment. Meredith told me that whenever I'm making an announcement or a decision, be as dramatic as possible.

"Well, I'm supposed to pick from the top two for lunch. I'd like to invite Hayden," I say finally, my heart pounding in my chest. More than a few faces drop, even though according to the rules, they'd already been disqualified.

Hayden's face breaks out into a grin as he starts walking toward me, his arms open wide. But I'm shocked when Meredith interrupts from the sidelines, shaking her head. "Wait! I'm sorry, Emily, but you weren't supposed to just pick like that. The crew was supposed to bring out the button for you to push. Don't worry, we'll edit that out."

I look at her, confused. "What button?"

As if in response, the crew quickly rushes forward and sets

up a prop button and the score displays change above us. The names *Hayden* and *Lee* flash back and forth on them, and apparently, when I hit the button, it'll freeze on one of their names.

Please let it be Hayden.

I stand and watch the names flash, concentrating. When I think I got a lock on the name I want, I smash the button and it freezes on . . . Lee. My heart drops in my chest and it's a struggle to keep the smile on my face.

I'm surprised when Hayden steps forward and gives me a hug, whispering in my ear, "It's all right, beautiful. Thanks for picking me when you had the chance. I'll look forward to our date." When he steps away, I have goosebumps on my flesh.

Before I can say a word, Lee virtually prowls toward me, appearing irritated and practically radiating power and sex. He takes my hand, kisses it softly with his lips, and then takes a little bow like I'm a princess. There's a challenge in his eyes when he straightens and looks at me. A challenge I don't think I want to accept.

"Shall we?"

CHAPTER 8

EMILY

Confessional

$\mathcal{I}$ look at the cameraman, sitting back in the high chair, feeling a bit of nerves tightening my stomach.

"Are we on?" I ask.

The cameraman, Joe, nods at me. "Talk whenever you're ready."

I pat my hair, hoping nothing is out of place and that my makeup isn't crazy, but I see McKayla over on the side give me a thumbs-up. I take a deep breath, thinking about what I'm going to say, and then draw myself up.

"Ahem." I clear my throat and begin speaking. "Never in a million years did I think I'd wind up on a show like this. I mean, I've watched enough of them to become an expert, but my experience being the first Matchmaker, thus far, has already been an eye-opener. The men seem nice, and it's been tough cutting some of them. There's a few I feel a spark with, so I guess we'll see how that goes. I appreciated Hayden's help with the bowling. There's a few I'm not as invested in, and some have even turned me off a little. I *work a lot with children, and I'm not looking for immaturity in a man. But who knows? Anything can happen."*

The comment gets a chuckle out of McKayla, and I continue. "I'm off to lunch with Lee, who seems very charming and confident. Other standouts? Matt . . . something in his eyes says he'd be fun to get to know more. Cody . . . uhm, he seems like a huge teddy bear and I kinda wanna cuddle up with him. Dean . . . kinda an All-American boy next door. Carlos . . . he promised to teach me how to dance, and that sounds fun. Yeah, there are some standouts."

*A*fter a quick touchup to my hair, makeup, and wardrobe, I settle in at an intimate table for two on the back porch. Well, it would be intimate if there weren't ten people around doing the set work. It's kinda funny when Meredith tells us that this is supposed to be a bit more revealing, more connection. She wants some kind of fireworks to happen.

Apparently, that's my job, like I have any idea how to create the 'camera magic' she's demanding. Lee, who's sitting across from me, is unaware of the turmoil wracking my mind as he smiles warmly at me. "I'm so happy to have lunch with you today, Emily. Finally, all to myself."

I return his smile, trying to relax and nodding my head. "Yes, I want to get to know all of you better to see who I might be a match with." I pause. God, I sound so awkward, so forced. It gives me a newfound respect for the women who seem so natural at doing these things.

"So, uh . . . tell me about yourself," I say, flashing a smile.

Lee grins, leaning back in his seat. "Well, I used to be a major gamer geek, doing live gameplay voiceovers. I moved on to a multi-media platform reviewer who gets early releases from the studios. As an early reviewer, my videos could make or break a game release. I've got about fifteen million subscribers."

I arch an eyebrow, impressed. Fifteen million and I've never heard of him? I have to wonder if he's pulling my leg, heavily exaggerating. But then again, I don't play video games or even get on social media much. "Fifteen . . . million?"

Lee smiles proudly, nodding. "Yep, my last E-Sports convention sold out within minutes. I had people lining up to watch me play and talk about the game." He goes on to tell me about how much he's made from endorsements and how he's headed for even bigger things.

I'm a bit flabbergasted, both in that I didn't even know such a thing existed and that he's talked for about fifteen minutes straight with barely a sound from me.

After a while, he must see something on my face, because he stops. "I'm sorry, I'm talking your head off. I'm just passionate about my work and can get carried away sometimes. You get the picture. Tell me about you."

I stare at him for a moment. I can appreciate that he's passionate, but I admit I'm comfortable steering the conversation away from something I know so little about.

At the same time, I'm hesitant to tell him about myself. I'm boring, certainly not *popular*. I could embellish a little, but I remember Meredith saying that I need to be truthful. She and the producers feel that viewers connect more with leads who are authentic.

"For the past few years, I've been working as a nanny. I was going to school for an education degree, and this was a way for me to spend time with little ones," I finally say. "I didn't expect to enjoy it so much, and while I'm still taking classes, it's on a more part-time basis so that I can take care of my kids when they need me there. They're like my family now, their parents too."

Lee grins. "So you're a babysitter? I think that's awesome. I'm sure you're great with the kids and they love you. Besides, who doesn't love kids?"

I shift in my seat. He's smiling, but for some reason, the way he called me a 'babysitter' almost feels like he looks down on it. I do so much more than that, but maybe it's just semantics. He probably just doesn't know the difference. I would probably botch video game lingo too. With a smile, I try to let it go, choosing to focus on the compliment he gave me instead.

We continue our lunch, talking about the show a little bit and what we dream about for our futures. When he says he wants a big family, I can't help it, my ovaries tingle a little as I like the sound of it. I don't know if he'd be the one to have that big family with, but if I were only a little more forward, I might just let him take me to bed to see if we're *compatible*.

I mentally laugh at myself. Like that would ever happen . . . yeah, that's not me.

Despite the wrong foot we got off on, I can't really find anything bad to say about Lee. He's been interesting, smooth, and he's even made me laugh a little. It doesn't hurt that he's easy on the eyes. It's been a lovely first date. Still, *babysitter*. The way he said it won't leave my mind. I think it wasn't the word that irked me so much. It was that his tone sounded a bit condescending. But nothing else has sounded that way. He's been quite charming and sweet, in fact, so maybe I should just let it go? Especially considering the stress of the awkward situation we're in.

As we stand up, Meredith pops up from the sidelines. I swear, that lady is a ghost Jack-in-the-box, popping up at the most inopportune moments.

"Great job, guys," she says, giving me a thumbs-up and a smile. "Just need the kiss and we'll call the scene." My heart jumps and my mouth goes dry.

Did she just say *kiss?* On the cheek, right?

I look at Lee, who's grinning like he expects to do more than just kiss me on the cheek. I don't know if it's because I'm being watched or what, but I feel unsure. I mean, I expected to be kissing multiple men. That's what the show is about, finding your perfect match. And you're sure as hell not finding him without getting your lips wet.

"Uhm, I don't usually kiss on the first date . . ." I reply. Shit, did I really just say that on camera?

Meredith smiles tightly at me like I'm a toddler, clearly not caring. "Prep for the kiss scene!"

I'm nearly shaking like a leaf as Lee steps up to me. He takes my hand, smiling at me. "I don't usually kiss on a first date either, but then again, we're both here for the same thing." He leans in and I close my eyes.

I'm expecting a bit of sweet smack, but Lee has other plans. He presses his lips against mine and then ignites, demanding entry and tangling his tongue with mine, his fists knotting my dress at my waist and holding me tightly to him.

Holy shit, my head is swirling and my knees feel like they'll buckle. I've never been kissed like this. After a moment, Lee slows down a little, pulling back, and I open my eyes. I can see the glint of satisfaction reflected in his as I suck in a gulp of air.

He watches me with a smile on his face, the corners of his lips turning up. He did go a little overboard, but I can tell he knows I liked it. As he releases me, I vaguely hear Meredith from far away. "Cut. Perfect. Let's head down for the match scene. Emily, you'll tell us whom you want to cut and then we'll do the ceremony."

Back in front of the hedge backdrop, I discuss my thoughts with Meredith, Nate, and his damn clipboard, going over everything about my date with Lee and the guys during the bowling. I tell them whom I'd like to keep and whom I'd like to see go, several times needing picture name cards to even know whom I was talking about.

Once we've made our list, Nate hands out the cards as the men begin to file in and stand before me with their hands held respectfully behind their backs. Every man looks a little nervous. Well, except two—Hayden and Lee. Lee is confident, and Hayden just looks a little upset.

It's because he wanted the date with me.

"Let's go!" Meredith yells from the sidelines, motioning at me like I'm a dog that won't obey his master. "Andele!"

Lowering my head, I suck in a deep breath and then let it out slowly. After a moment, I raise it and let my eyes roam across all the gathered faces. "Gentlemen, I had so much fun on our group date today. Some of you showed that you were true sportsmen and consummate gentlemen. Some, however, didn't. Unfortunately, I'll have to send some of you home tonight." I let out a dramatic sigh, frowning. "I want you to know it's really hard for me to make these choices so fast, but

I have to decide based on the time we have. Please don't take it personally . . . you're just not the perfect match for me."

I look over to the sidelines, where McKayla and Brad have shown up. They're both grinning at me and giving me thumbs up.

I tear my eyes away from them, even though their presence and support give me confidence to keep going in some weird way. "So, without further ado, Lee. We had the date together, and it's time to see if we're a match."

Grinning like a wolf that's caught his prize, Lee walks up to me with his card.

"Ready?" I ask.

Lee nods. "Yes, ma'am."

He turns his card over at the same time I do, revealing our split image on both cards. I give him a radiant smile. "Lee, we're a match."

He grins, giving me a hug and whispering in my ear, "Thank you, gorgeous," and goes back over with the group of men.

I swallow, keeping my eyes neutral just like Meredith instructed so the viewing audience won't know whom I'm picking next whenever this airs. I work down the rest of the front row of men. Mark, Luke, Shawn, and two more guys who just haven't stood out are cut.

And then there were ten.

CHAPTER 9

HAYDEN

*F*resh out of the shower, I run my fingers through my hair, checking for stubble on my jawline. Yesterday was rough for me, having my chance with Emily snatched right out of my hands. What made it even worse is that Lee got the date instead.

"How do you think their date went for real? I don't believe a word that douchebag Lee says." asks Dean, the guy the producers have me rooming with. He's standing next to me at the double vanity, slicking aftershave lotion along his cheeks. Dean seems like a cool guy from Colorado, somewhat laidback with a wicked sense of humor. If we weren't competing, I might enjoy having a beer with him. Actually, I probably still would. I'm a big boy and can deal with a bit of competition.

"No idea," I respond, turning to face him.

"What do you mean?" Dean gawks in disbelief. "You heard Lee last night after their date, going on about how awesome it was. He even said she's a good kisser, just a little skittish at first, but apparently, he 'warmed her right up'. He's such a player. Wouldn't be surprised if he finger banged her while the cameraman wasn't looking."

Just the thought of such a scenario unsettles me, but I brush the image away. I don't really know Emily yet, but I know enough to say that she has class and wouldn't do something like that on a first date with a man she doesn't know.

I shake my head. "Not a chance. One, Emily isn't like that. Two, Lee's the type who would brag, so he'd have already shared that with everyone like a cocky asshole."

Dean arches an eyebrow. "Okay, you're right about Lee, but how would you know she's not like that? She seems like a nice enough chick and all, but you don't even know her. She could just be here for the fame and is willing to fuck her way to the best match."

I give Dean a look to let him know this isn't a conversation I want to have. "I've seen enough to know she's not like that."

He gets the point and turns, running some product through his hair. He's got a pretty conservative cut that totally makes him look like a regular dude. "Well, Lee's one lucky bastard either way. First impressions are always big."

I'm not going to lie. I hate the fact Lee got the first date with Emily and that she chose to keep him around afterward. It couldn't have been bad if she kept him afterward. It didn't help matters that he bragged about the date before the ceremony, making us all a little nervous, and then after, he went around acting like he's already a shoo-in to win. Just around us guys, of course. I'm not so sure he's telling the truth, but I haven't had my time alone with her yet.

When I do, this whole game will change.

"Can't believe we're doing horseback riding," Dean complains when he's done messing with his hair. "I've never even touched a horse."

"Well, Emily spun the wheel, so now we have to make the best of it," I say, finishing my grooming. Last night, in another one of those moves that makes reality TV anything but, Meredith announced that our next activity would be horseback riding but we needed to film a scene of Emily spinning a wheel so it looks like a random selection. Yep, reality TV is totally real . . . and if anyone believes that, I've got a bridge in Arizona to sell them too.

After going down for the makeup they make us wear for TV, they make us get dressed in *Western* gear for full effect. The Ruff Ryder Jeans company is a sponsor of this episode, so we all line up for a camera scan of our asses with their logo prominently displayed.

It's no big deal for me. I've done it thousand times before. I just go over to the fence and flex my glutes in a way I know makes my ass look good on camera. This should really only take a few minutes, but they keep having to adjust some of the other dudes' poses.

While I'm waiting, I feel a tingle on the back of my neck. Glancing back, I catch Emily staring straight at my ass. The corners of my lips curl up as I lift an eyebrow at her. She doesn't even realize I see her at first, but then she blushes when she realizes she's caught. She looks so damn gorgeous in her cowgirl gear.

She's wearing tight blue jeans that hug her curves, show-casing her ass and thighs. Her hair is loose and flowing in beautiful shimmery waves with height at the crown of her head. For a moment, all I can think about is her hugging my hips with those thighs as I tangle my hands in her hair. *Mmm, ride me, cowgirl.*

I start moving toward her, my legs seeming to move of their own volition.

Unluckily for her, she gets pulled away by one of the makeup crew. I think his name is Brad. He's whispering something in Emily's ear, but I see her shooting glances my way.

We wrap up the shoot and start the horse training as a group. With so many of us, it takes forever, and almost an hour later, we've been fully versed on mounting, dismounting, sitting properly on our horses, and guiding them with the reins. I feel like I've got a bit of an advantage. It can't be a lot different from riding a Harley, can it?

We all ride along, Emily in the front just behind the lead horse. One by one, each suitor rotates riding next to her, getting a few moments to chat and make an impression. I can't wait until she narrows us down so I can get some real time with her. I'm just biding my time, being patient, knowing I'll shine when I get my chance.

When it's my turn, I ride forward and lock eyes with her. "See something you like back there?" I ask playfully. "I could arrange a private viewing."

Emily blushes, but she doesn't look away, nodding while laughing. "I sure did. Brad and I were just talking about Carlos's ass."

I chuckle. We both know she's full of shit. "Uh-huh. You're a terrible liar."

Emily laughs, lowering her head. "All right, you got me. Maybe I was checking out your—ahem—assets." Without letting go of the reins, she teases me by lifting both hands in front of her like she's squeezing melons, and I imagine her squeezing me like that . . . as I pump into her.

My jeans suddenly feel tight as I reply, "It's like that, huh? Take a squeeze anytime you like."

Her blush deepens as I hold her gaze steady for a moment. "You look pretty comfortable riding. Have you been around horses before?"

I can tell she thought I was going to make a dirty joke about her riding me or something, and I admit it did cross my mind. But there's a fine line between flirty and crude, and something tells me Emily is a good girl and might run from anything too over the top. I don't want to push too far, too soon. I'd like to get to know her before she gets the wrong impression of me. Gotta take it slow and easy so she doesn't startle, just like these horses.

She ducks her head and the sunlight hits her face in a way that looks like she has a halo. God, she's fucking beautiful. "Yeah, I used to ride at summer camp as a counselor. I helped the kids get over their fear of horses. I'd take them up trails and then we would find clearings to ride in."

"That sounds like fun. I bet you're everyone's favorite camp counselor," I say sincerely.

She looks at me, surprised, and eyes me for a moment like she's trying to figure out whether I'm playing her. "Most folks think I'm crazy for being around kids all day like that. I do admit, teenagers can be like demons from hell sometimes, but they're not all like that." A soft smile appears on her face. "Most are looking for validation in some way, attention, and they want to be listened to. I love to be the one to do that for them."

The emotion in her words pulls at my heartstrings. I can tell she's not just saying it for the cameras. She really does love what she does.

"You make me wish I had you as a counselor when I went to summer camp," I say. "And I'm not saying that because you look good in a pair of jeans, although you most definitely do. All the counselors I had just wanted me to sit down, shut up, and finger paint."

Emily blushes and laughs, and I admire how sexy she looks sitting on the horse. She's a natural. "Well, since we're practically the same age, that'd be a little hard. But there you have it. It's therapeutic for me, and it's what led to my being a nanny. I can't wait until the day I have one of my own."

As she talks about children, her eyes alight with passion, I'm moved. She's more than beautiful on the outside. She's angelic inside too. "I can tell you enjoy what you do. The kids are lucky to have you because that love and patience is a rare combination. The world could use a few more people like you," I say truthfully.

Emily stares at me slack-jawed, but before she can respond, I hear Meredith yell, "Next! Let's move it along!"

Gritting my teeth, I curse the woman in my mind so my chest mic doesn't pick it up. Meredith always seems to interrupt just when things are getting good.

Brushing away my irritation, I dip my chin, tip my imaginary hat, and smile. "I enjoyed the ride, Miss Emily, and I look forward to our next conversation. And no, I'm not saying it because of the game."

Emily's responding smile is like a ray of sunshine.

After the rest of the guys have had their time, we stop for a picnic lunch on a patchwork of blankets spread across the grass. Some of the guys are cautiously hanging around the edges, but there's a large majority trying to get Emily's attention without being overbearing. It reminds me that this, regardless of the connection I feel between Emily and me, is part of a game, and I have to be willing to play.

Lee somehow snakes his way to her side and I'm forced to listen to them talk. He's saying all the right things, but my bullshit radar won't stop going off. It's more than just what he's saying when we're off camera. There's just a sense of oiliness about him. If I found out he read a book entitled *What to Say so Girls Will Fuck You*, I wouldn't be surprised. The way he talks sounds that practiced, like this is a stunt he pulls in bars every weekend. He probably doesn't respect Emily or any woman.

Seeing Emily laugh at something he says makes me grit my teeth. It irritates me that she doesn't seem to see what I see. Or maybe she does and is just playing nice for the camera, but she's keeping him around for a reason. I've never been a man to get jealous, but I can't stand the sight of the two of them together.

Chill, I tell myself. *His fake ass charm is going to become evident soon enough. If she doesn't see Lee's true colors yet, she will eventually.*

After lunch, we head back to the barn and see the TV screen and button setup. Meredith orders us all around it.

"It's time to announce who the lucky winner is for the date with Emily," she says, smiling naughtily, which heightens the anticipation. "Private time in the hot tub!"

There's a murmur of excitement around and Emily blushes furiously. My heart is pounding like an iron fist in my chest at the thought of one of these assholes getting half naked with her.

Looking around, there's one I don't want her with more than the others. Lee's confident grin as Emily walks over to the screen rubs me the wrong way. No way this fucker gets chosen again.

"Start it," Emily says. Her chest is heaving with anticipation, but I don't know if it's because she's nervous or if it's because she's looking forward to being with one of us in the hot tub.

Names begin to flash across the screen, all ten this time, decreasing my odds. I watch with bated breath. It *has* to be me.

Time seems to slow to a standstill as I watch Emily reach out and press the button. At that moment, I close my eyes for a second and then open them a second later.

My name is on the screen and Emily is smiling a mega-watt smile right at me.

CHAPTER 10

EMILY

Confessional

"*How do I look?*" *I ask Brad, who's eyeing me from the side. He's just finished doing a little touchup.*

"Fierce, bitch! Fierce!"

"We record in ten seconds," says Joe behind his camera.

I quickly rearrange my outfit and clear my throat.

Joe raises his hand out to me. "3-2-1-and go!"

I smile at the camera as if I'm reminiscing about the date from heaven as I speak.

"So, my date with Lee went really well, better than I expected. We had some good conversation and he seems like a passionate guy . . . and he capped it all off with that kiss. Like, I've never been kissed like that before.

Besides that, the horseback riding was fun. I'm glad I got to talk to each guy for a few minutes alone to get to know them. The one who stood out the most for me was Hayden, though. I just love his personality! I've never been around a guy that hot, with his whole bad boy vibe, but he can actually carry on a conversation that's genuine. And when he's talking to me, it's like he's lasered in on me and I can feel it in my bones. I want to find out more about him next time I get the chance."

I sigh as if I'm talking about my Prince Charming rather than a contestant on Matchmaker.

"I don't know if it's too early in the competition to be catching feelings for someone, but I definitely feel like I have a connection with Hayden. And the sound of his voice whenever he says my name . . ." I close my eyes and let out a little girly squeal. "He's just like . . . walking sex on a stick."

"I can do this," I tell myself, running my hands down my sides and examining my body. "He's hot, sexy, and he actually likes me. Who cares what anyone else thinks, viewers at home or otherwise?"

I'm feeling pretty good, considering I'm about to go on national television in a fucking barely there bikini. Fuck it, I'm lying. I'm nervous as hell for two reasons. One, because viewers will see all of my body, and two, I'm about to get into the hot tub with the sexiest guy I've ever seen. It feels strange to think this, considering how hot and sexy so many of the guys are. Lee's close, too, and the way he kisses . . . wow. But Hayden has some type of raw magnetism that pulls me in.

Before changing, McKayla curled my hair into some amazing mermaid waves and Brad added a hint of turquoise right at the outer corners of my eyes.

For the swimsuit, it's a white bikini encrusted with silver sparkles from some corporate sponsor of the show. I asked about it being sheer when it gets wet, but Meredith assured me that if there was even a hint of nip, they'd edit it out.

At least it's covering me and doing some flattering things for my curves.

"Action!" Meredith yells, ripping me out of my reverie.

From my hiding place off camera, I take a calming breath, standing tall to walk onto the mansion's patio, and I nearly gasp at the lovely twinkle lights hanging above like a private sky of stars. The crew has gone into great detail to make the setting as romantic as possible, even setting up a line of rose petals leading to the tub and beautiful thick candles on small tables nearby.

Hayden is standing by the hot tub, looking like he just stepped out of a gym, in simple black board shorts and his rock-hard abs on display. I watch as his eyes nearly devour me as he looks me up and down, but I gotta admit that I'm looking him up and down the same way.

In that moment, I feel sexy, wanted. Something I never feel because I've always been too busy with helping children to nurture my love life. And God, am I turned on by Hayden's hot body.

But I try not to let it show, even as a wide smile takes over my face like a giddy schoolgirl. Despite anything going on internally, I intend to flirt like no one's business and give the viewers what they want. Sexy, flirty times.

And is he who I want? Abso-fucking-lutely.

I place my hands on my hips, swishing back and forth a little as I throw his earlier words back at him. "See anything you like?"

Hayden swallows thickly, his eyes glued to my body, giving me a surge of confidence. "Fuck, yes, I do."

I place two fingers to my lips, looking mildly alarmed. "Can we swear like that on this show?"

"Don't know, don't care. They can edit it out." His voice is low, almost feral, and it sends sparks down to my nether regions. "C'mere, Emily, let me see you closer."

It's not a request but an order, and I react without even thinking, moving toward him as if he's put me under a spell. He starts walking toward me too, and we meet in the middle. He grasps my hands, holding them out wide, and turning me around to get a good look at my figure.

A low whistle of appreciation escapes his lips. "Emily, you look stunning. Like an angel in white, so I guess that makes me the devil in black?"

"Stop it." I blush, trying not to stare at his hard abs and barely resisting the urge to run my fingers down them. I swear it's gotten super-hot all of a sudden, and I'm damn-near naked.

"You started it." He lets go of one hand, bringing his palm up to gently cup my cheek as he looks me in the eye. I think he's about to kiss me, but then he whispers, "We getting in this hot tub or am I going to have a situation I'd rather not share on camera?"

My cheeks burn all the hotter as he bites his lower lip. "Let's do it."

Grinning, he leads me into the tub. The water is warm as I sink down and it sends my temperature up a notch. We sit side by side and he offers me a glass of champagne that's conveniently waiting on a small table next to the hot tub.

"So, tell me more about yourself," I say, fingering my glass and focusing my eyes on his handsome face. "I feel like you have a lot to tell."

Hayden takes a sip of his champagne and then sets it aside. "Hmm . . . where to start?" He scratches at his jaw, lost in thought, and I watch him over the rim of my champagne glass.

Clearing his throat, he finally says, "Well, when I was younger, I thought I was the shit. I had everything going for me in high school—good grades, girls, and baseball talent scouts showing up at my door." He lets out a mirthless chuckle, and I see a twinge of pain in his eye. "I even had a college scholarship to play at one of the big baseball universities. All things pointed to me making it to the big leagues." He goes silent, a shadow passing over his face.

I stare at him, on the edge of my seat. "And what happened?"

Hayden sucks in a breath, and though he's looking at me, his eyes are a little glassy, lost to the memory as he relives it. "It was the second round of the state playoffs, and we took the lead into the sixth inning. I was playing right field that game. Coach wanted me to rest for the state finals before pitching again. One of their batters tagged a low fastball, sending it long toward me. I went running for it and jumped to get the catch. Went over the wall and landed on my right shoulder."

I gasp, my stomach clenching. "You got hurt."

Hayden nods, looking vulnerable for the first time. "My rotator cuff, when I least expected it. I thought for sure, there was some way it would heal, even if most of them don't fully, and I did everything I could to keep playing. I adjusted my throwing motion, rehabbed like a madman . . . anything I could do, I did. I knew how my parents were depending on me and how badly they wanted to see me achieve my dreams, but in the end, I had to give up the sport. It just wasn't working."

Tears sting my eyes. "Oh . . . that's so terrible. I'm sorry."

Hayden nods, clenching his jaw. "Shit happens. And I'm not going to lie, I was depressed for a while. But I'm over that now." He shrugs nonchalantly. "Moved on to a new chapter of my life."

Though he's trying to put up a bold front, I know Hayden is lying through his teeth. The injury still bothers him. Even now.

Is that the reason he's here? says a tiny voice of doubt at the back of my mind. *Is he trying to regain some lost former glory?*

I push away the troublesome thoughts and ask, "So how's that chapter been? What do you do now?"

Hayden grabs his glass of champagne and takes another sip. "My next career move came completely out of the blue. I was visiting campus to apply for financial aid when a modeling scout approached me. At first, I was like, dude, are you coming on to me? Because he would not stop going on about how beautiful I was and kept trying to touch my hair and squeeze my biceps. Not exactly the approach I was used to getting."

He pauses, and I laugh as I picture him strutting onto campus, a little down but hopeful to get to financial aid, encountering a random guy wanting to run his fingers through his hair.

He continues, "Once I realized he was offering me a modeling job, I figured it was a scam hook for porn and he just needed some fresh young meat. Eventually, he convinced me he was legit, and now he's my agent."

"Wow, so a model, huh?" I ask as I look him up and down with a grin. I motion toward his arm and tease, "May I?" He smiles and I give his arm a little squeeze like his agent wanted to. "Yep, I can see it. I'd buy whatever you were selling."

I'm pleasantly surprised when Hayden blushes. Maybe he's not as cocky as he'd have me believe. "Thanks. It's been a change, that's for sure. Dad used to come to every single one of my games, even cried when my shoulder quit on me." He chuckles. "He's all right with my modeling, but he does like to give me shit about how he can't understand who would pay to see my ugly mug."

I giggle. "Dad knows what's up, right?"

Hayden huffs, his cheeks turning light red. He must be getting more than a little hot. Part of me wonders if it's partly due to being close to me, or due to the hot tub? "Right," he agrees sarcastically.

We fall into silence for a moment, the sound of the hot tub motor and rushing water filling our ears.

"I've always dreamed of being a teacher," I say, breaking the quiet. "It's been the one goal I've been working toward before coming here."

"That makes perfect sense with how much you love kids," Hayden says.

"Yeah, but it sucks when I can't be the teacher I want to be because I can't afford to go to school full-time. So I settled for being a nanny instead. Not that I don't love my kids and my job, of course, but I looked into those scholarship programs, and I even applied for several. But they don't cover luxuries like food and water, and coordinating a part-time job and an internship is impossible. So I take a class or two each semester, but at that rate, it'll be years before I finish. So . . . I compromised."

Hayden tilts his head, looking at me in a way that makes my skin prick. "I don't know. To me, it doesn't sound like you settled at all. It just sounds like one path to your dream wasn't a possibility right now, so you found another way to be happy and do what you love." He moves in, running a hand down my shoulder and causing goosebumps to form all over my body. "That's what I like about you. You're resourceful."

Along with sending my temperature up another degree, that simple compliment makes me beam like a girl who got her first hula hoop. Not only is Hayden drop-dead gorgeous, but he just seems to get me. And he's focused in on me in a way that none of the other guys, including Lee, have been when I'm alone with them. I just feel it.

We continue our conversation, finding out little tidbits about each other. As we talk, it seems like we drift closer and closer to each other. It's not long before my legs are resting across his as he absently strokes them in the midst of our conversation.

It doesn't feel sexual, but sensual . . . almost like a massage. The more we talk, the more comfortable we feel. And I just can't seem to stop staring into his beautiful blue eyes, taken by how they seem to pull me in and devour me in their depths.

"So yeah, Dad wasn't . . ." Hayden stops what he's saying, his eyes on my face.

My heart jumps in my chest. I was engrossed in his tale about his dad coming home to find that Hayden had taken some of his baseball cards. "Did I turn into a frog or something?"

Hayden doesn't reply, simply reaching out and moving a strand of hair behind my ear in a gentle fashion.

In that moment, I feel like I'm drawn to him like a moth to a flame. And not even Satan himself can keep me away.

In slow motion, we move toward each other, and he pauses barely a breath away from me, teasing the moment, making me realize how much I want him to kiss me. And then he does and it's magic.

Pure. Fucking. Magic.

He's powerful but not overwhelming, licking gently across my lip, asking for entry. Our tongues tangle with each other and I hear a moan, realizing its me. He pulls me the rest of the way into his lap, and I feel his hard cock pressing against my hip.

From what I can tell, he's huge and absolutely turned on by our kissing. I groan softly as I feel his hand threading through the hair at the nape of my neck, gently fisting it. And his other hand comes up to my cheek, his thumb rubbing across my cheekbone as he breaks our kiss, bringing our foreheads together.

I'm lost in him for a moment, wanting to be nowhere else but here. I could drown in him right now and I would curse the person who dared try to save me. I'm his.

Just as I'm about to lean in to kiss him again, I hear the hated,

"Cut!" Meredith is smiling from offset and I'm amazed that I forgot about the camera and the people lurking quietly in the dark around us. "Great job, guys."

Uh, Meredith, can you kindly shut the fuck up, please?

Hayden seems to be thinking the same thing as we give each other a little smile, still a little breathless. Neither of us wants this to end, and it shows, but we manage to climb out of the hot tub and Hayden pulls me in for one more hug.

Right before I pull away, he whispers in my ear, "Thanks for the great date. I'm gonna dream of you, that kiss, and your hard little nipples in this bikini all night. Look what you do to me . . ." and he releases me, stepping back.

I look down and . . . oh my God. He might be covered by a layer of black nylon, but he's so fucking hard for me right now. My eyes meet his. "Sweet dreams, Hayden. I know I'll definitely have some myself."

CHAPTER 11

HAYDEN

Confessional

"*Y*ou ready?" *Joe, the cameraman, asks as I finish buttoning up my dress shirt. It itches a little. They barely gave me time to rub down with a towel before herding me in here half dressed.*

"*Hold your ball sack," McKayla Quinn growls at Joe as she finishes combing my hair back. For my first confessional, she popped up and said she'd be fixing me up so I don't end up on TV looking like ass crack. Her words, not mine. "I'm almost done."*

"*And I'm almost ready to tell Emily she can forget about this one," Brad Cooper, the make-up artist, says as he steps back and peers at my face, practically salivating for me. "There's a saying—too hot for TV—and this fine piece of man is definitely pushing that line."*

I try not to laugh as the two artists finish and begin bickering with each other on the sidelines. After I check myself over once, I give Joe a nod and he begins the countdown to taping.

"*I don't think I can find enough words in the English vocabulary to* describe Emily," I say, staring straight into the camera and giving my best smile. "She's smart, sweet, funny . . . and undeniably sexy. I just don't know what it is about her, but I find myself having the best of times whenever we're together.

"Learning about Emily on our first date really showed me what a great person she is. I love how much she lit up when she talked about helping kids and how much she wants to be a teacher.

"But damn, when she put on that bikini." I shake my head. "Listen, I know I'm supposed to be a gentleman and everything but . . . she's fucking hot."

I give myself a look in the mirror before I hustle out of my room into the suitor's hall to head down to breakfast.

It's mad early for breakfast, but since ending our date, I've felt like I can't get my mind off Emily. As I'm rounding a corner, I see her, dressed in a tank top and shorts, her sexy legs on display, heading into a door ahead. A grin spreads across my face as I rush up the hallway and sneak in behind her.

I try to be quiet as I come through the door, but Emily immediately senses my presence, and she turns around with a gasp, her eyes as wide as saucers. "Hayden, what are you doing in here?"

I know I shouldn't, but I can't help myself. I move in closer, crowding her body with my own. Her breathing slows, becoming heavy and a little ragged. In that moment, I know she wants me. It's only my enormous self-restraint that keeps me from seeing just how far I can push it.

"I dreamed of you last night," I tell her, my voice a soft growl. "And I wake up today, walk out of my room, and here you are, right in front of me like a figment of my imagination. I had to follow you to see if you were real."

Emily bites her lower lip and looks away for a moment, blushing. "I might've thought about you last night too," she admits. She spreads her fingers inches apart to indicate just how much. "Just a little."

Desire courses through my veins as I move in even closer. "Oh, really?" I growl. "And what did you think about?"

She's practically shaking, and the corners of my lips curl up into a grin as she searches for words. "Nothing. Just . . . our date."

I arch an eyebrow, placing a hand on the small of her back and pulling her closer. "Are you sure that's all?"

"Y–yes."

She's lying, but it doesn't matter. I'll let her off the hook.

"I had a great time talking to you yesterday," I say, "and you know . . . after."

"After?" Emily asks breathlessly. The smell of her desire is in the air, her warm, lush body making me hot as hell. "What do you mean—"

I lose control of myself, giving in to what we both want. If we get caught, damn it all. At least I can go home a happy man. I close in, kissing her passionately, and with a growl, I pull her to me by her hips. The feeling of her ass under my hands is electric and my cock surges to full hardness, sandwiched between our bodies.

She moans, her hands moving over my shoulders to tangle in

my hair at the nape of my neck. Spreading her legs slightly, she grinds against me. She already wants it hard and deep, and I'm more than happy to oblige.

Kissing down her neck, nibbling and licking, I move my hands to cup her breasts, teasing her already hard nipples. I slip the strap of her cami tank top off her shoulder and suck her nipple into my mouth, teasing it in tight circles with the tip of my tongue. "Oh, God, Hayden," she whines in my ear, trying to be good but unable to help herself. "Hayden . . ."

I move up, whispering in her ear. "As hot as it is to hear you say my name like that, we need to be quiet. Can you be quiet for me?"

Emily nods, biting her lip to keep herself quiet, and I lower back down, sucking her right nipple into my mouth, rubbing and pinching the other. Pulling back, I catch her eye. "Emily, I need to touch you. God, can I touch you?" She dips her head once, and I slip a hand up the loose leg of her shorts, cupping her pussy through her cotton panties. "Mmm, you're soaked."

Emily nods wordlessly in reply as I slip a finger into her panties, pulling them to the side, and run my finger across her delicate folds. So hot and wet, her pussy almost feels like warm caramel. Emily can't hold back her soft moan, her hips pressing forward, searching for more. I ease my finger into her, curling up toward her front wall. In and out, I press, adding another finger to fill her and using my thumb to rub across her clit. "Hayden, I'm so close. Don't stop."

I feel her tight pussy squeeze as she gets ready to come, and just in time, I cover her mouth with mine, muffling her cries as I feel her coat my fingers with her orgasm. I keep swiping my thumb across her clit, prolonging her pleasure until she bucks at me, letting out a big, happy sigh. When it's over, I pull back, looking into those wide, sexy eyes. "That was the sexiest fucking thing I've ever seen."

Emily smiles, shaken by the intensity of what just happened. "Wow . . . that was—"

She stops mid-sentence as she realizes I've moved my fingers from inside her to my mouth, sucking at her juices. I meet her eyes and let her watch as I run my tongue around and around. "Sexiest fucking thing I've ever tasted too."

She smiles, moving forward to kiss me. After a moment, she seems to remember where we are. "Shit. McKayla and Brad are gonna be here any minute!"

I help her adjust her clothes back, and just as I meet her lips with mine for a goodbye kiss, the door opens behind us.

"Girrrrlll . . ." a high falsetto voice gives me half a second of warning, and I turn around and see McKayla and Brad, both of them grinning at us with matching raised eyebrows.

She points to each of us as she speaks. "All right, we are supposed to be in here. *She* is supposed to be in here. But you are not supposed to fucking be in here."

Brad smirks, his eyes glued on my crotch a little too much for my comfort. "Or be fucking in here."

Emily is turning redder by the moment, stammering to cover up what just happened. "No, uh . . . we were just talking about our date last night."

"Don't even try it, naughty girl. Even I know what a just-Oed woman looks like. And it's . . . that." He pauses, moving his hands around, indicating Emily's entire body. "I can't blame you, though. He's hotter than a habanero tamale."

I have to do the right thing and try and keep Emily out of trouble. "Look, I'm sorry. It's not Emily's fault. I snuck in here to talk to her. Don't rat on her, okay?"

McKayla and Brad look at each other, then McKayla speaks up. "What are your intentions with my girl here?"

Her girl? Interesting. "Uh, aren't we all here to see if we're a match? Last night was great and I just wanted to tell her that. One thing led to another, just not what you're thinking."

McKayla gives me an appraising staredown for a moment, and I can tell she's running me through her bullshit detector. With a nod, McKayla steps away from the door. "Uh-huh. Well, y'all got damn lucky there's no cameras in here or you'd be all over the production room right now."

I feel Emily jerk. "Oh, God, I didn't even think of that."

McKayla smirks. "Mmmhmm, must've been other things on your mind. From here on out, do the dates, see if you're a match, and skip the impromptu outings. Capiche?"

I nod once at McKayla and turn to Emily. "I'm sorry about that. I'll see you in a bit for our date?"

She nods, and I figure we're already in deep, so I lean in, meeting her eyes, and cover her mouth with a quick kiss. Moving to her ear, I whisper, "Sexiest fucking thing ever."

With a smile, I slip out the door, hearing the immediate chatter start behind me as McKayla and Brad laughingly interrogate Emily. "Bitch! Tell me everything."

As I make it down the hall, I can't help but smile. That was awesome, even if it could've gone really wrong there when we got caught. But I wouldn't change a thing. Well, maybe if we'd ended with me filling her body with my still-aching cock until she moaned my name into my ear. That would've been better. We'll have to be more careful next time. Because there's damn sure gonna be a next time. With that promise made to myself, I head out to meet the rest of the suitors and the production team for today's date setup.

CHAPTER 12

"Why, you dirty slut, you!" Brad exclaims when Hayden is gone, shaking his head as if I've been caught with my hand in the cookie jar. "While we've been sleepin', you've been creepin'!"

"Girl, he must've done a number on you," McKayla says, coming forward to place her hands on my shoulders and shaking me like I stole something from her. "Is he as good as he looks—"

"I bet you rode him like you rode that horse the other day," Brad cuts in over her, coming up to my side and causing McKayla to shoot him a deadly glare.

I break free of McKayla and smack my palm to my forehead, letting out a groan, my face burning. "Guys, please. It's seriously not what you think." They didn't really see anything, but I'm still more than a little embarrassed at what I'd let him do. But fuck, it felt so good, and my head's still spinning from it. "We were just talking and then he kissed me."

Brad makes a face. "Uh-huh, sure. We've all heard that

before. Next time, you'll say you just happened to walk in his room and tripped to fall right on his dick."

"Actually, he followed me in here," I say defensively. "It was only for a second." I try to sound as convincing as possible, but I know I'm probably failing.

They exchange looks and become quiet, plunging the room into silence.

"I'm guessing you must really like Hayden," McKayla says quietly after a minute. She sounds different, not as bombastic, almost as if she's wistful.

I slowly nod my head. "He's been nice so far. I like him more than I thought I would, actually." Oh, God, and does he know just how to make me squirm.

I can tell Brad is just itching to crack another joke, but he shows restraint. "Does that mean you have already made up your mind?"

"No," I say, and then I quickly add, "At least I don't think so. Hell, I don't know. I feel so confused right now. I think this is going to be a lot harder than I thought it would be." I wrap my arms around my waist and squeeze, feeling a mix of emotions. "But yes, Hayden's definitely in the lead."

"Don't you think it's a bit early to decide?" McKayla asks. "Sure, Hayden's hot as hell and all, but so are those other men out there. You could be missing out."

"Exactly. I didn't say my mind is already made up," I say. "Besides Hayden and Lee, I haven't really gotten to know anyone else yet. They could be totally awesome, maybe even the man of my dreams." I sigh.

"Mmmhmm," Brad mutters under his breath like he's not buying it.

"Well, just continue to keep your options open then. For the show's sake and for yours," she says. "You don't want your preference for Hayden to come out on tape or the viewers will pick up on it and kill the suspense. Not to mention, it might irritate Meredith."

I nod, realizing that regardless of whether anyone knows what went on in here, there could be consequences if Meredith found out that Hayden and I were alone together. "Guys, please don't say—"

"Our lips are sealed," McKayla says, following my train of thought. "Aren't they, Brad?" She gives him a look, practically telling him what to say.

Brad nods. "No one will hear a peep out of me! You're just lucky he didn't follow me in here instead. You'd be out a suitor."

Despite my trepidation, I let out a laugh, feeling a sense of relief. "You two are the best."

After getting me ready, we leave the room and head down for another Matchmaking ceremony. As we walk, I'm so trying to not get too hung up on the way Hayden made me come this morning, but damn if it's not impossible to keep the satisfied grin off my face. I was about two seconds from getting on my knees for him before I remembered where I was.

Once on set, we start with another round of card matches to let four more guys go, Archie, Liam, Daryl, and Ron. I feel bad as I watch them walk off, muttering amongst themselves. I'm glad the numbers are starting to wean down, though. I'm making cuts faster than Freddy Krueger. With fewer suitors, I'll have more time to get to know them and I won't have to just go with my gut and cut guys I've barely spoken to.

Thankfully, Meredith agrees with me on my choices, saying they were boring. Of course, that's all she cares about.

When we're finally done with the ceremony, I'm left with six suitors. Now it's time for today's 'game', although I quickly learn that I'm not supposed to do much more than be eye candy, which isn't as much fun as I'd hoped. I step up to spin the activity wheel and it stops on football. At Meredith's direction, Nate divides the guys into two teams of three.

With a grin, Meredith says, "Cut! All right, bring them in."

A group of young boys and girls comes in, and although I'm smiling warmly, I'm confused as to why they're here.

Meredith points at the men while the children giggle in the background. "They're here because they will help make up the two teams. They'll be playing touch football, and the winning team gets a group date with you. Emily, you're to be a cheerleader for both teams, but maybe one suitor more than the others?" She asks like she's leading me, and I panic for a moment. Oh, God, please don't tell me that Hayden and I were on camera.

I cast a guilty glance to the sidelines to where Brad and McKayla are watching, but McKayla simply shakes her head. Next, my eyes fall on Hayden, but he appears calm and collected, only giving me a soft nod of reassurance.

Meredith stares at me and makes me feel like she's about to accuse me in front of everyone when she finally puts me out of my misery. "What, no favorites yet? Well, production definitely has favorites, so we'll see how it plays out."

I let out a big sigh of relief. She doesn't know.

We head out to a big backyard area that's been spray-painted to resemble a football field. It occurs to me that Meredith had to know the wheel would land on football to have the kids on set and field ready. And the same is true of the horse-back riding yesterday, but I was too caught up in Hayden's jeans-covered ass to give it much thought. Just how 'random' are these supposedly random computer-controlled choices, anyway?

Of course, I knew there'd be some element of set-up to the show, but that seems pretty planned out and gives me a moment's pause. If they're orchestrating the dates, what else are they pulling the strings on? Before I can dwell too much, the game starts. The team quickly named *Fire* has Hayden, Matt, and Dean, while *Diamonds* has Lee, Cody, and Carlos, each with a gaggle of boys and girls ready to play. "Hey, why Diamonds?" I ask.

Lee grins and calls back. "Because we're a girl's best friend!"

I turn to the other team. "And you guys?"

"Because our hearts burn for you!" the three guys all call back in unison, making me blush as Meredith grins from the side.

The teams run back and forth, the guys trying to protect the children as they run for touchdown after touchdown. It starts off pretty casual, and as the score goes back and forth, everyone is still giggling well into the third quarter. As the fourth quarter starts, the score is Fire-49 / Diamonds-42. I can tell that the suitors are a little more serious now, especially with such a close score and a small group date on the line.

Their smiles get a little dimmer as tension forms in their

faces, and I see Lee saying something to Hayden that obviously makes him angry.

On the next play, a little girl on Lee's team has an opening, and Lee scoops her up, dashing for the touchdown. Once they're safely in the end zone, he spins her around, smacking her hand with a high-five. It's perfect and adorable, making me smile as the girl runs back for the huddle.

My smile falters when I see the look on Hayden's face. Even if they are competitors, whose heart wouldn't melt at the sight of that? I can't help but wonder what has him so upset. With a check of the clock, there's only a couple of minutes left.

Both teams line up, and when the play starts, the smallest boy on Lee's team intercepts a pass by Dean. He's off to the races, running as fast as his little legs can go while Lee does what he can to block for him. With unexpected speed, he makes it all the way to the end zone.

"Diamonds win!" someone yells from the production area near the scoreboards.

All the kids explode with excitement and I find myself cheering just as loudly as I rush into the crowd, caught up in the excitement. The tiny boy is up on Lee's shoulder, taking a victory lap like the MVP that he is.

The two teams line up, walking past each other for high-fives and handshakes. It looks like Lee and Hayden smack each other's hands just a little harder than necessary. I try not to let the image bother me as I follow down the lines, high-fiving all the players, suitors and kids alike, with a smile plastered on my face.

From the sides, Meredith waves her arms, yelling, "Cut!

Great job, everyone. Emily and the Diamonds team . . . hang back, and I'll let you know where you're going for the group date. Everyone else, off set."

Almost immediately, the mood dims as everyone realizes this is a competition. The kids seem a little confused at being hustled away, but Hayden seems to catch it. "Hey, guys, I know our fridge has a ton of hotdogs and ice cream. Who wants to have a little post-game barbecue?"

The mention of ice cream has a few of them screaming, the mood back up, and even a few of the production crew smile. Everyone walks off, leaving me with Lee, Cody, and Carlos. The look Hayden flashes me as he walks off, one of resigned defeat, nearly makes me want to chase after him and join him for the barbecue.

But Meredith walks up, looking between all of us, ready to give orders. "All right, this is going to be exciting. You'll be going bungee jumping. The car leaves in one hour, so get ready!"

Suddenly nervous, I look at the guys, who all look back at me. They don't look quite as scared as I am.

"Have any of you bungee jumped before?" I ask. "I'm kinda freaking out . . . not sure if that's good or bad."

Cody, a tall blond who looks like he's been imported from Scandinavia, chuckles. "Not sure if they've got a rope that'll hold me. I went with some buddies once and I was too tall and too heavy for them to let me jump. Life of a linebacker, I guess."

"I haven't," Carlos and Lee both say.

"Ugh, so we're all newbies," I groan. "No one to assure me that everything's going to be okay."

I try to keep my smile on my face and pretend like I'm having a good time as we walk back toward the house. I'm nervous. I'm not exactly the risk-loving adrenaline junkie type. Just thinking about having to bungee jump has my stomach queasy.

I'm so preoccupied with my thoughts that I don't notice Lee slithering up next to me, putting his arm around my shoulder. "New experience for both of us, huh?" he asks.

I jump, causing him to chuckle.

"Don't worry, I got you." He grins, pulling me a little tighter.

I flash him my fake smile. "I'll be okay, but yeah, I'm a little nervous."

"They say intense situations like this make you get close to people faster," he says softly. "I'm sure that's exactly why they have us doing this. And I have to say" —he leans in closer to whisper conspiratorially— "I bet you're not as nervous as those two girls over there," he says, pointing at Cody and Carlos.

I feign a laugh and lightly swat at his arm "You're so bad. They're your teammates and helped you win."

Lee shakes his head. "Nah, I'm pretty sure that ringer of a kid got us that win today. One of the other kids said he was an All-Star PeeWee player. I couldn't quite picture it with his size, but it seems to have worked out in my favor."

Lee's being sweet, and I love how he let the kids play out there. It could've easily turned into a macho fest, and I smile genuinely at him.

We reach the porch steps, and the guys say their goodbyes, all promising to see me in the car.

Lee stops, coming in close. "Emily, I had a great time today, and I think it's just beginning." Before I can react, he quickly leans in and presses his lips to my cheek. I'm a little surprised at the boldness out in the open, but the kiss is over almost before it began.

With a wolfish smile at the look on my face, Lee turns to head in, leaving me feeling more than a little bit confused.

CHAPTER 13

HAYDEN

I head into the house with Matt and Dean, all of us disappointed that we lost but pretty stoked after a fun morning with the kids. Even with missing out on the group date, it's hard not to smile at their excitement. The production crew stepped in while we were heading back to the house, and they're going to get catering to set up an impromptu barbecue outside in twenty minutes.

Still, I can't stop thinking about Emily. Our moment we shared has been the only thing on my mind since this morning. If it weren't for this whole charade, I'd have had her screaming my name by now. Then again, if it weren't for this show, I probably would've never met her. But I can't stop thinking about how she felt and when I can feel her again.

I grit my teeth as I remember Lee's slimy smile. During the fourth quarter, I had to bite my lip when he taunted me. "Don't worry, it'll all be over soon, and she'll be on my cock . . . right where she belongs."

What he said was crass enough, but something about the way

he said it sounded so condescending, it made me want to punch him right in his smug face even more. He doesn't respect Emily. He's doing this for the fame, for his Instagram fans or something. She can't see it, I don't think, but I can understand. He's playing the cameras just right. Of all the men left, he's the one I'm most concerned about being able to win her heart because of his bullshit façade.

"Well, that sucks," Dean complains as we all flop down on the couch. Sitting next to him, I prop my feet up on the large ottoman in front of us. "I thought I was finally going to get my time to shine. Nice save on the party idea though."

He's my competition, but I get Dean's frustration. Whatever his real reason is for being here, he's not an asshole. Or maybe I'm just biased because we have a mutual disdain for Lee.

"You're not the only one," mutters Matt, who's sitting across from Dean. He looks over at me. "Speaking of which, how was your date? What's she like? We're here competing for her and I've hardly had a chance to talk to her."

Despite my irritation, I grin. "A gentleman never tells."

Dean lets out a laugh, kicking my foot off the ottoman with his own. "Dude, you're so full of shit. You're seriously not going to tell us?"

I chuckle. "You'll find out for yourself soon enough."

At that moment, all of our heads swivel simultaneously as Lee comes strolling in, all swagger and attitude, with Cody and Carlos behind him.

"Too bad, guys. Us . . . winners . . . are off for a day of on-camera bungee jumping while you sit around wanking off and wishing you were us," he sneers. His eyes are on me as he says it and it takes a colossal effort not to jump up and make his face a part of the furniture.

Before I can reply, Dean snorts. "Trust me, Lee. If I'm wanking off, you're the last fucking thing on my mind."

Matt laughs, eying Lee up and down. "I don't know, dude. I might let Lee rock my fantasy world. He seems like he could take a pounding."

For once, Lee looks at a loss for words, a range of emotions crossing his face. "Dude, what the fuck did you just say—"

Matt interrupts him. "Calm down, asshole. I'm just fucking with you. I'm not really going to make you my bitch."

Lee shakes his head while the rest of us try not to laugh. "Well, gotta get ready. Don't want to disappoint my fans. I'm up another half-mill followers since I got here. Need to keep making those good impressions on Emily too, if you know what I mean. We've got a connection," he says, bringing his hands together and interlocking his fingers. With a cocky smirk, he walks out of the room toward his bedroom.

Watching him go, Cody and Carlos shake their heads, having been silent during the whole exchange.

"Holy fuck, if we could switch places," says Cody, clenching his fist so hard his massive knuckles pop like small firecrackers. "I'd let either of you go in my place just so I didn't have to put up with his fake ass. I'm gonna have a hard time not calling him out on his shit. Knowing my luck, I'll probably come out looking like an ass on camera."

Carlos nods, looking like he wants to chase Lee down. "I know. I might be a dog, but that guy is just downright wrong. All sweet and sexy to Emily and when the cameras are rolling, then a crude douchebag any other time."

Carlos and Cody both give us a nod, then head off to get ready while Dean and Matt decide to change t-shirts before the barbecue. I hang back, sipping on a Coke and thinking.

I've got to see Emily again, I think to myself. *If only there were a way to see her off-camera.* I feel like I need to warn her off Lee, but mostly, I just want to get to know her better without the cameras. Suddenly, I have an idea.

McKayla said we were lucky there were no cameras in her room, so she has to know where the cameras are. She can get a message to Emily for me. It might not be the best idea, but it's worth a shot.

Jumping to my feet, I head back down to Hair and Makeup, running into Nate in the hall.

He looks at me with surprise, blinking rapidly behind his wide-rimmed glasses. "Where you headed, Hayden?" he demands.

I grin, trying to appear like I'm not up to something. "Oh, just to the kitchen. Our mini-fridge is out of water and I wanted to hydrate before the party."

Nate peers at me for a moment before sighing. "Really? Well, I'm sorry about that. I'll let catering know immediately." Scribbling something on his clipboard, he scurries off.

I watch him leave and then continue on my way. I get to the room and knock once before stepping inside and closing the door behind me.

McKayla, who's messing with a wig while Brad complains about his feet being too big and wide to fit into Emily's heels, spins around in surprise. "Oh, hell no!" she snaps, shaking her head. "You can turn your hot ass right back around and get the hell out. Emily isn't here and you're not supposed to be either."

Brad smirks, kicking the high heel to the side and flipping his hand at me. "Speak for yourself, hooker. I don't mind at all. As long as he's willing to show some of his . . . assets. Squats? I bet you do squats, don't you?" he asks as he tilts his head, analyzing my lower half.

I'm not sure whether to laugh or not, so I just ignore him and look directly at McKayla. "Look . . . hear me out. You said earlier that there were no cameras in here. That means you know where they are. I need to talk to Emily, no cameras, no production crew, just us. Can you help me with that?"

If looks could kill, I'd be roadkill right about now, but I stand my ground. "Please."

McKayla scowls at me. "And why would I do that? You're asking me to risk my job. Just wait until the show is over and talk to her all you want . . . regardless of who wins. I'm not going to let you drag me into this mess."

"I can do that too," I say, "but . . ." I pause, at a loss for words. This is frustrating.

Brad leans forward. "What's your game plan?"

"I like her," I say. "She's—"

Brad rolls his eyes. "No shit, Sherlock. That was obvious when we busted in on you two doing the Twister—"

"She's smart, funny, and I want to talk to her for a few minutes, not try to play with her emotions just to win the show like some of the guys who are left. Which reminds me, she should probably know a few things," I continue, talking over Brad. I stop, surprised at how much I said as McKayla and Brad go silent.

McKayla looks me up and down, then bends her head toward Brad and starts whispering. I stand there uncomfortably, hating how foolish I must look.

McKayla pipes back up. "Fine, you've got balls. I like that. Not a rule follower. I like that, too." She stops to scowl darkly at me with warning. "But if you hurt her or ruin this opportunity for her, I will take those big balls of yours and snip them off with the dullest pair of scissors that I have. Questions?"

It takes great effort not to start laughing in her face. This chick is seriously one card shy of a full deck, threatening me with that dark look on her face but then brightening right back up at the end. Mood swings, much?

I shake my head, keeping my tone serious. "Nope. No questions. So, what can you tell me?"

McKayla taps her ruby red lips with her fingernail. "Hmm, inside the house is tough. There's cameras in almost all the rooms you can access except the toilets. Not particularly romantic. Ah, the pond . . . how do you get there without being seen?"

I watch as her mind whirls, not interrupting. She's nuts, but she's smart and devious. I like it.

Brad suddenly lets out a squeal, raising his hand like he's trying to get the teacher's attention. "I got it!" he exclaims excitedly. "Out the side door to the smoking area, you know that place where you can pop through the big hedge?"

"Holy shit!" McKayla snaps her fingers, smiling at Brad. "You're a genius! I would kiss you if I knew it wouldn't turn you into a flaming hetero who wanted me day and night." She snaps her finger, strutting around him.

Brad rolls his eyes, unfazed by her backhanded praise. "Bitch, please, you could be the last pussy on earth with the human race depending on us to procreate and I still wouldn't get within ten feet of that. You forget, I know where it's been."

"So anyway," she says after a moment of glaring at Brad. "On the other side, y'all can go down past the back lawn area, to the trees at the back of the property, and then sneak up to the private pond back there. It'll just be you and the ducks."

I grin, happy to find a resolution "Perfect. Thanks." I pause. "What time will it clear out and be free of security guards?"

McKayla lets out a hum, thinking. "Guards don't patrol back that far, but they might catch something on the monitor when you slip through the hedge."

"Don't worry about that," Brad says. "Slip through right at the eleven o'clock shift change, and I'll swing by to tell Harvey about my date last week. He loves hearing about my escapades. He claims he's straight, but it's so obvious. Getting back in won't be a problem. People always rag on him because he's asleep at the monitors by two. Just come in separate doors, at least twenty minutes apart, and it'll look like you're both just having trouble sleeping and decided to wander if you do happen to be seen."

McKayla nods. "I'll let Emily know when she comes in to get her makeup cleaned off after the group date. But I have to warn you. If she's not interested, you're on your own, buddy."

I flash a wolf-like grin of confidence. "She's interested," I say.

At least that's what I have to tell myself.

I nod my head at them as I prepare to leave. "Thanks, ladies," I say before quickly adding, "And, uh, gentleman. Sorry, Brad, no offense."

Brad laughs, waving me off with a wink. "None taken. I'm more of a lady than Pinky Pie Hooker over here could ever think of being."

With a wink, it's all set. Just hours and hours to go until show time.

CHAPTER 14

EMILY

"So, what are those kids you babysit like?" Lee asks me as we go over a bump in the road and I nearly fall into his lap. "From what I could tell before, they seem like a big part of your life."

It's barely an hour after the football game ended and I'm already loaded up in a large SUV with three guys, still feeling nervous about the bungee jumping.

"Oh," I say, feeling my worries slip away at the mention of Mindy and Oliver's kids. I even forget the camera that's sitting right in our face. "They're absolutely wonderful! The boy is just like his father, smart and practical. The girl is just like her mother, funny and sassy! And their baby . . . he's got the world's softest little tummy and still loves to cuddle. Together, they can be quite the handful, but I wouldn't trade being with them for the world."

Lee grins, leaning forward. "You really have a strong bond with them, don't you?"

I nod. "I do. They're like a second family to me, the little brothers and sister I never had. We do a lot together." I start talking all about my past with them, telling funny stories about things they've said and how smart they are.

As we pull into the lot, I suddenly realize that I've monopolized the conversation this entire time.

"I'm sorry." I blush, feeling ashamed for gushing so much when I was just thinking Lee did the same thing before. "I didn't mean to go on and on."

"Shh," Lee says softly, placing a finger to my lips. "Don't do that. Your face lights up when you talk about them and it only makes you more beautiful. You'll be a great mother one day."

I can't help the smile that forms on my face at his compliment, even if the touching on the lips was a little awkward in front of everyone. Despite my reservations about Lee, I'm really flattered. But as I glance around, I see Cody and Carlos smirking at each other with a hint of eyeroll. Are they jealous that Lee is so sweet?

I can sense that something is off between the three of them, but I decide to just roll with it since I'm not sure what it is. I'm only getting glimpses into what these guys are like. And it's possible they just don't like each other because of the unusual situation we're all in. I'm sure the competition stuff is hard for them to handle and still be friendly with each other.

We climb out of the SUV, heading in for the lesson before we can jump. Turns out, Cody was right. He's both too tall and too heavy for the bungees they have for this jump. Carlos teases him a little bit, but Cody takes it in stride saying he was just along to spend time with me anyway.

Cody takes my hand. "You cheered for us this morning, so I'll cheer for you this afternoon. It'd be my honor," he says, ducking down like he's bowing, which puts his face roughly at my level. He lifts his eyes to mine. "As long as you scream my name on the way down."

I laugh. Cheeky, but polite about it.

I like him, just enough sarcasm to keep me paying attention without being cruel.

Meanwhile, Lee says he hasn't been bungee jumping before, but he seems to be comfortable with the whole setup. Although I'm sure he'd never show any sign that he was nervous. But it still puts me at ease that he's so confident with something that is quickly turning my knees to jelly. We line up on the bridgeway, the coolness of the height sinking into my bones as a slight breeze makes my eyes water. Or maybe I'm crying in fright . . . I'm not sure.

Lee makes his way over to me. "Kiss for luck?" he asks with a boyish grin.

I hesitate for a moment, Hayden flashing before my eyes, but then I remember the rules of the show and what Meredith expects from me.

Just give him an innocent peck.

Hiding my anxiety, I smile, raising to my toes to kiss Lee's cheek, but he turns at the last moment, catching my lips and holding me in a seemingly deep kiss while he presses his hand to the back of my head.

Caught by surprise, I feel myself pulled into his chest, realizing the camera is right there, almost in the kiss with us.

Lee smiles down at me, running a thumb across my bottom

lip. My lips tingle, and I look up at him, my heart pounding in my chest.

He stage-whispers in my ear, "I think I'm buzzing more from you than I will be from this jump." And with a full-wide smile, he lets the instructors lock him into the harness, hooking the bungee to him. He steps up to the edge, and with a countdown of 3, 2, 1 . . . he's gone with a joyous yell.

Feeling sick, I peer over the edge, following the line of the red bungee to see him swinging far below the bridge, and I can hear him screaming, "Yeah! Whoo!" with his fist pumping in the air.

I smile. He survived and seemed to have fun. I can do this too, right?

Carlos is up next, and after a pleasant kiss to each cheek, his jump goes just as well, although he seems to be screaming in Spanish on the way down. Not sure what he said, I overhear Meredith telling Nate to make a note for subtitles and bleeping for his scene. Carlos is smiling though, and he flashes me a thumbs-up.

Now it's my turn.

I stand on the edge, strapped into the harness and attached to the bungee, looking over the edge of the bridge to the river slowly running below and the trees along the riverbank. It's a beautiful view and I think I'd be just fine to stay here and enjoy it.

Cody comes up next to me when he sees me frozen. "You got this," he says.

I look at him with wide eyes, nodding. "I don't know," I whisper. "It'd be nice to just hang up here."

"You can if you want," Cody says softly, reassuringly. "You don't have to jumps if you don't want to. And yeah, I'd enjoy hanging out with you while they reel those two up. But consider this . . . when are you going to get a chance to do it again? If you step down, that fear is just going to grow. But right now, you're already here, strapped in safe and sound on a perfect fucking day. Take a big breath and jump, enjoy this moment of your life, and inspire all the other folks on the other side of that camera to tackle their fears. But most of all? Inspire yourself to do it . . . bungee jumping and whatever else scares the shit out you. Do it. Chase those nervous butterflies because that means you're challenging yourself and growing."

I stare at him slack-jawed. It's by far the most words he's said while on the show, and here I was this whole time thinking he was a giant airhead. "You're pretty good at pep talks," I say. "Experience with that, I take it?"

Cody nods. "I've given more than a few when I played ball, and I've heard some that have inspired greatness. Em . . . you're gonna do this and do great."

"Hurry up!" Meredith yells, uncaring how scared I am of jumping off this bridge and landing flat as a fucking pancake.

"Looks like that's your cue," Cody says as I bite my lower lip. "Don't worry, I'm not going to throw you off."

With a smack on the ass that somehow feels more friendly than sexy, I turn to the wind.

I can do this.

From far away, I hear the countdown . . . 3, 2, 1 . . . and I'm flying! The trees suddenly look more vivid, the river looks faster, and the wind is howling through my hair as I plunge down below, screaming my lungs out. The rebound hits and suddenly, I'm on the way back up before floating weightless for a second and dropping again, the process repeated four times before I settle down at the bottom of my cord.

When it's over, I'm shaking like a leaf, adrenaline rushing through my blood. It was absolutely awesome and the scariest thing I've ever done at the same time.

They wind me back up, and when my feet touch down on the bridge, Cody is whooping with me, grabbing me in a big bear hug that lifts my feet a foot off the ground as he jumps around with me.

I'm laughing, delighted at his reaction.

After a few more yells, he sets me down and looks me in the eye. "Hey, I forgot to get my good luck kiss!"

I look back at him and he lowers way down, giving me a warm kiss that makes me smile. He pulls back with a smack and grins. "And don't think I didn't notice that you didn't yell my name. Guess I'll have to make you yell it another time." He winks at me, letting me know that he's joking . . . a little.

The drive back to the estate is full of laughter, everyone talking about their jumps and how their minds were racing with fear and excitement.

When we get back, Meredith and the camera crew are waiting for us to step out of the SUV.

"Okay, say your goodnights," Meredith orders, "and then you're done until early morning." She looks at me pointedly. "Except you, Emily. I need a confession from you before you turn in."

The guys wait their turn to tell me goodnight, Carlos giving me a hug and a light kiss on the cheek and Cody picking me up in his strong arms to bring me to his level for a quick smattering of kisses, and then I'm alone with Lee.

Of the three, Lee is the most aggressive, moving in close and crowding me up against the SUV.

"I had a great time today, gorgeous," he says, his voice a soft growl. "You were brave, jumping off the bridge. it looked like you were flying. It was so sexy to see you be such a badass." He stares at me with such intensity, and I'm not sure what to make of it.

Before I can reply, he kisses me passionately, his tongue slipping in to tangle with mine as he fists my hair in his hand, moving me where he wants me. I feel the length of his body against mine and feel his cock surging against my belly. He grinds against me for a moment, groaning, and it's such a sudden onslaught that it takes me a moment to process.

I push back against his chest lightly. "Lee . . . slow down."

Lee breaks the kiss, breathing heavily. "Sorry," he rasps. "You just drive me crazy. I want you so much."

Off to the side, I hear Meredith furiously whisper to the cameraman, "Did you get that? Please tell me you got it!"

"Of course I did."

I quell the irritation that surges in my stomach, hating that nothing is private. It's been days, and it's still hard getting used to the cameraman always being there. He's just around so much that I sometimes forget he's even there until afterward.

I'm too preoccupied with my thoughts to reply to Lee, so he lays one more kiss, this time to my cheek, before pulling away and walking toward the house. "I'll see you tomorrow, babe."

I stand there like a statute, feeling all sorts of emotions going through me.

Holy shit. What just happened?

Lee just overwhelms me and I don't know how to feel about it.

"*Bungee jumping was amazing," I say with a smile as I look into the camera. "I don't think I could've done it without Cody. He really stepped up to cheer me on when I was terrified and doubting myself. He was such a good sport about not being able to jump himself, too.*

"Lee is . . . intense. I feel like he's sweet, but when he kisses me . . ." I shake my head, momentarily at a loss for words. "It's just powerful. The football game was awesome to watch. The kids were great, and I was sad there had to be a losing team, but it was really cool about the barbecue afterward. It seemed like there was some animosity between Hayden and Lee, but they're both big personalities, so I guess that makes sense."

Meredith interrupts from the sidelines. "Hey, Emily, need a little more about how hot the guys looked playing football."

I tear my eyes from the camera. "What? What do you want me to say?"

"Just play up the fuckable factor, m'kay?" Meredith demands. "That is, if any of them were. At least just say who caught your eye."

I let out a sigh before plastering a big, fake smile on my face. There was one person who stood out to me the most.

Confessional, Take 2.

"The football game was awesome to watch, and the guys all looked hot as hell," I say, pretending to fan myself. "And they were amazing with the kids. I guess Hayden caught my eye the most out on the field. He seems to be a natural leader. After the game, he took his shirt off, and can you say abs? I caught a glimpse of his tattoos. I'd like to see those closer because I couldn't really see them in the dark when we were in the hot tub. I'd like to find out the story on those."

As I talk about Hayden, I come alive, my words just coming out so easily they don't even sound fake. Whenever this segment airs, there's not going to be a single person watching who doesn't believe my attraction to Hayden.

When I'm done, I turn and flash a smile. "How's that, Meredith?"

Meredith smiles and nods her acceptance.

CHAPTER 15

"Are you two out of your mind?" I say immediately to McKayla and Brad, shaking my head. We're in my dressing room, and I haven't even had a chance to get out of my clothes good before they tell me about Hayden's plans to get me alone. I'm shocked, to say the least, but a part of me is more than a little intrigued. "It's too dangerous."

"I hear what you're saying," Brad says, who's wearing his blond hair in two tiny pigtails and has his eyes framed by dark eyeliner, "but your voice and your body language are saying something else entirely! It sounds more along the lines of *I want to ride his big dick again.*"

"Stop that!" I snap, trying not to laugh. "I'm serious. I did no such thing!"

Brad stops and gives me a look. "Okay, I'll let that go. But please, don't tell me you didn't at least *think* about it."

McKayla, who's dressed in a purple dress with a white belt at the center, rolls her eyes as she tosses a bristle brush she was using to groom a wig to the side. "Enough, Brad, she's right.

Stop messing around." She looks at me. "Look, Emily, I'm just the messenger. It's your decision. You know better than me if he's worth the risk." She gives me a smirk that says *he's totally worth it*, even if she doesn't outright say it.

McKayla and Brad just look at each other and smile, as if they know I'm going even before I do. "All right," I say without even realizing it. "I'm going to go see him."

What did I just say?

There are so many things wrong with sneaking around with Hayden without the cameras, the main one being violating my contract and putting the entire show into jeopardy.

Not that I haven't violated my contract already. Oh, God, what he did to me with just his hands. I can only imagine—

I stop my thoughts. That's not happening. We're just going to talk. I swear, talk is all we'll do.

"Great!" McKayla chirps. "Now go get yourself a shower while we get ready, and then come back here so we can make you look like a princess deserving of her Prince Charming."

Thirty minutes later, I'm fresh and clean, dressed a lot differently than I have before as I furtively move through the halls. Mckayla wanted to have me all dolled up again, but I admitted that I wanted Hayden to like the real me, not just a fake TV version, so this is a bit of a test to see how he reacts to my more natural look. My hair and makeup are soft, like something I'd wear back home, and I borrowed a simple red cotton dress from wardrobe. It's a little short but more sweet than slutty. Despite my anxiety, I feel an air of confidence about myself, recognizing that this is the most 'me' I've been in days.

I turn a corner before doubt hits me like a freight train.

"Should I really be doing this?" I mutter, pausing in the middle of a hallway somewhere near the back of the estate and peering back down the way I came. So far, I haven't encountered any crew, but if they see me back here, I'm fucked. Sure, I look somewhat normal, but I'm not supposed to be in production areas.

This is a dream come true, and I'm putting it all on the line just for a few minutes alone with a man I've talked to only a handful of times.

But honey, those hands . . .

I should turn around and head right back where I came from. But I'm not going to, and I know it. All it took was one thought of how he made me come. I still can't believe I did that. It's so not me, but it almost felt like we had a true connection. Although maybe it was just lust and nothing more.

Ugh. But I seriously want to get to know him, dammit!

I'm just confused. Lee turned my brain into mush with a kiss just a mere few hours ago. The way he looked at me sent me whirling, and the world still isn't quite straight on its axis yet.

Jesus, what the hell am I turning into?

I usually kiss on the *third* date and am shy about doing anything more than that for ages. That is, with the few guys I've actually dated long enough to have sex with. Today, I went on a date with three guys and kissed all three of them. Now, I'm sneaking out to see a fourth, whom I've already let finger bang me.

A part of me feels slutty, even if it was all part of the show. Well, at least the date with three men part. But I feel like meeting Hayden is what I want to do. It's the most real thing about this entire show so far.

I circle back, making sure I don't encounter any crew. I walk out the side door off the den, stretching and breathing like I'm getting some fresh air while I look around, checking for witnesses.

Seeing nobody, I quickly slip through the hedge, doing my best to not get tangled in the branches. I curse when a few scratch my flesh, but thankfully, they don't break skin.

As soon as I'm through, I see Hayden. He's pacing back and forth as if he's uncertain I'll show. My heart pounds as I watch him. I'm so not a rule-breaker. It makes this so much more exciting.

Still, the part of me that always does as I'm told wants to run away, and the other part wants to run straight into his arms.

He sees me before I can do either.

"You came," he breathes, his face lighting up as he comes forward to pick me up and spin me around as he covers my lips with kisses. "Holy shit, you're beautiful," he says in awe when he's done, stepping back to survey my outfit. He shakes his head. "And you smell good, too."

I grin, blushing at his praise and excitement for me, my lips burning from where his touched them. "You like it? It's a fragrance Brad picked out for me." I make a face. "I think he called it *Lush Lust*."

Hayden laughs, shaking his head. "He and McKayla are something else." He grabs my hand, tugging me off into the darkness. "Let's go."

We quietly make our way down the hedge line to the trees.

He leads me deeper into the trees for a moment, scouting ahead to make sure the coast is clear and then coming back to escort me forward.

When we step out to the pond, it takes my breath away. The moon reflects off the surface, giving the ripples a sparkling effect. I know it sounds cliché, but it looks absolutely magical.

Holding my hand, Hayden leads me to a blanket he's laid out next to the bank, and we sit.

He shakes his head, a grin coming across his face, his eyes glowing in the moonlight. "I'm so glad you came," he says, the relief in his voice genuine. "I wasn't sure you were a sneak-out-to-see-a-guy kind of girl. I got the impression before that you were the one who always followed the rules. I think I like that you're a little naughtier than I thought you were."

I laugh. "I'm really not. This is the first time I've ever snuck out . . . for anything. But I'm a grown ass woman. I can do what I want."

Hayden chuckles. "That you can." We sit in silence for a moment, the chirps of crickets filling our ears, enjoying the scenery for a few moments. "So what made you decide to be on *Matchmaker*?"

I purse my lips, thinking. "Honestly? I'm a bit of a boring homebody and a reality TV show addict. I saw a commercial promising adventure and experiences on the season finale of a show and figured I'd give it a shot. I never expected them to pick me or even call me back." I let out a mirthless laugh. "What are the odds that they'd pick me?" I shake my head. "But I knew it was probably the only shot I'd ever have at being on one of the shows I love, so I went for it. And look, it paid off."

"Why *wouldn't* they pick you? A beautiful, unsuspecting woman who finds love on the show? It's a perfect story. All the rest of the women who get chosen to come on here are going to have mighty big shoes to fill."

I blush. I love the way Hayden's words make me feel. "You think so?" I ask.

"I know so," Hayden says confidently. He leans forward, his eyes alight with interest. "Tell me more. What do you love about reality shows? I mean, this has been fun, but it's all a little too fake, don't you think?"

The mirth flees my face as I nod. "Yeah, there's that. Well, I knew things would be scripted, so that's not really an eye-opener for me. At home, it's just an escape. I feel like I get to know the people based on their reactions to whatever situation they're thrown in. It's interesting to see how people deal with different things. Although I did think there'd be more getting out and adventure, from the way they described the show to me. Today was a start, I guess." I look over at Hayden. "What about you?"

Hayden sits back on his ankles. "Well, before I showed up here, I had a little issue with a photographer wanting a bit too much from me. Instead of flipping out, I walked off-set with him yelling in my ears. It was unprofessional, but I wasn't about to do what he was asking." A faint smile plays across his handsome face as if he's remembering something. "That was when my agent told me he got me an interview for this show. I didn't want to do it at first because I can't act for shit, but Jay, my agent, pulled a guilt trip number on me and I slowly changed my mind. After a while, I didn't think it would be so bad. Like you said, it's reality TV and they're just looking for true reactions, so I thought maybe I could handle that." He laughs, scratching at the stubble on his chin.

"Apparently, they needed a guy who fit the whole bad boy biker asshole profile."

"You don't seem like an asshole to me," I say softly, looking him in the eye. "You've been nothing but sweet to me."

Hayden chuckles. "Woman, if you think I'm sweet, I'm gonna have to up my game. I notice you didn't comment on the bad boy biker part?"

I grin at him mysteriously. "Yeah, well, I don't know anything about that since we're kind of told what to wear and I haven't seen any bike. But a bad boy biker sounds like fun."

Without warning, I move to him, lifting my head, inviting him to kiss me. His lips barely touch me at first, soft and gentle, but there's already such heat between us that the softest touch ignites the blazing fire within us. We're soon kissing each other hotly, our tongues dueling as we claw at each other's clothing.

He lays me back, kissing and sucking down my neck, one hand coming up to cup my breast, his thumb rubbing across my nipple. Hayden purrs in my ear, sending another thrill through me and taking my breath away. "Mmm, Emily, I could kiss you all night, but I've been thinking of how you tasted all day. I need you on my tongue again."

Hearing the agreement in my moan, he works his way down my body, helping me slip my dress top and bra off and suckling on my breasts as he pushes my dress down further, taking my panties with it. I lift a leg to get them the rest of the way off, and he leans back, taking me in with his eyes. Hayden clears his throat before he can speak. "Fuck, woman, perfect . . . you're perfect."

He covers me with his body, and it somehow feels even

135

naughtier that I'm naked while he's dressed. We writhe together for a moment, and I need to feel his skin on mine. I reach for the hem of his shirt, encouraging him to take it off. He lifts his arms, and I slide it up and over his head, kissing his lips hungrily when his mouth is exposed again. When I see his bare chest, I can't help but touch him, pressing the palms of my hands across his hard pecs, tracing down his abs. I look over his ink wonderingly. "I want to know the story of each of these," I tell him, tracing his tattoos.

"Anytime, anything you want to know," he says before capturing my hands and pulling me close again. He returns to kissing my neck as he rubs and tweaks my nipples. Just when I think he's not going to say anything, he starts murmuring in my ear. "The roses on the fronts of my shoulders have baseball leather and stitching in the petals. I got the flaming compass one when I had to start from scratch. Burn everything I knew and go in a different direction."

I meet his lips, exploring his mouth with my tongue. "Okay, tell me the rest later. I thought there was something else you wanted to do with your tongue?"

I smile shyly and he grins back at me. "Oh, trust me, I didn't forget . . . but we have all night." With a lust-filled gaze, he runs his tongue from my sternum, down to my belly button, dipping in for a moment that makes me giggle, and continuing on down to lap at my pussy. My hips jerk. He's so good at this that I'm losing control almost immediately, and he's only just beginning. He licks and sucks at my clit, fucking me with his tongue, then slips first one and then two fingers inside me. "Fuck, you taste so good. I could die a happy man with your taste on my tongue."

I groan without even realizing it. Hayden hums hungrily in response, his tongue fluttering quicker over the tip of my clit.

I clutch at the blanket as he starts curling his fingers, rubbing me and setting my nerves on fire as my hips take over, bucking up into his voracious lips and smearing my juices all over his face. "Hayden . . . oh, fuck."

"Anytime," Hayden says breathlessly, and I throw my head back, holding back my screams of pleasure by pure luck alone. Hayden holds me to his lips until the last spasm is gone before withdrawing his fingers and kissing his way back up my body to find my lips, kissing me softly as he takes me in his arms and rolls me on top of him. I sit up, reaching down to undo his pants. Hayden lifts his hips and I slide his pants down, my eyes widening at what I find. "Surprised?"

I gawk, reaching down to ease his underpants down over the bulge in front of me. He's perfect, just like I knew, and my mouth waters at the idea of returning the favor he's given me. Leaning forward, I lick the head of his cock, and it's velvety smooth and warm, with a ridge behind his head that I tease with the tip of my tongue. Hayden wraps a hand through my hair and pulls me back, his breath coming in short gasps.

"You keep that up . . ." he says, reaching with his other hand into his pocket. He takes out a condom, and I understand, grinning.

"Well, now you know how I feel," I joke, unwrapping the condom and easing it down his shaft. "Next time, I want more of that."

"Next time, huh?" he says, taking my waist in his hands and holding me over him. "I like the sound of that. Now . . . let's ride."

The first touch of Hayden's cock against my pussy makes me want to drop down hard, satisfying the aching throb inside me, but his powerful hands keep me frozen, unable to move downward as he lets my wetness coat the condom. When I'm just about ready to beg, he starts lowering me, my body stretched and filled like I didn't know was possible. I groan, glad he took the time to ease himself inside me. When I'm all the way down on top of him, Hayden looks up, pulling me down for a deep kiss. "How's it feel?"

"You know damn well that this is amazing," I reply, squeezing my pussy around him. "You're perfect."

Without saying anything else, I start to ride him, rolling my hips back and forth, letting his cock fill me and thrill me. Hayden holds his hands on my hips, squeezing my ass and thrilling me as he looks in my eyes the whole time. My ass bounces up and down on his cock, slapping hard against his upper thighs as I drive myself faster and faster until Hayden starts thrusting up into me, meeting my hips with his own and driving the breath out of me. It's gigantic, each upward thrust of his cock meeting my hips and making my clit grind against the base of his cock and sending explosions through my body. I try to maintain eye contact until I can't take it anymore. "Hayden!"

He rolls us, pinning me to the blanket and pushing my knees up until they're sandwiched between our bodies, and he takes total control, pounding me mercilessly. I'm unable to move, totally in his control, and I love it. His power is undeniable, and the sensations sweeping through my body make my toes curl.

"Em . . . Em," Hayden grunts sexily as his cock plunges in and out of me. I feel him swell, and with a harsh grunt, he comes, the last thrust pushing me over the edge. I feel the explosion start somewhere between my pussy and my stomach and catapult outward, my body shaking as I cry out. Hayden covers my mouth with another kiss, muffling my cries to make sure I'm not heard. We're far away, but with how that felt, who the hell knows?

When our bodies can finally relax, Hayden rolls off my body, his cock slipping out and leaving me feeling empty and already wanting more. Still, I can barely breathe, and I let him hold me as the night air cools us to the point I can speak again. "So, now what? What do we do?"

Hayden strokes my hair and chuckles softly before kissing my forehead. "Well, I guess I'm gonna need to be damn sure I'm your match."

I chuckle and nod, content to stay in his arms all night. But eventually, our whispered chatter slows as we know we need to get back before we're caught. We dress and head back to the house, Hayden walking me to the hedge by the side door. I can see his dark silhouette as I sneak in, walking toward my room and trusting that he'll stick to the plan and come in another door in a little while, no one the wiser.

CHAPTER 16

HAYDEN

$\mathcal{I}$ sip my black coffee, wishing I could mainline it as I sit in a chair in the lounge, gazing out at the landscaped grounds. Early morning call time has me more than a little grumpy, along with everyone else.

Being out late with Emily is one thing, but even after I successfully snuck back in, I was so pumped I couldn't sleep. There's just something about being with her. Yeah, we've got chemistry off the charts, but it's more than that. I want to talk to her, listen to all the thoughts that run through her brain, and experience life with her. And I met her on a damn TV show, of all things.

Thinking of Emily makes me wonder where she is and what we'll be doing today. I get the answer to one of my questions a moment later as she comes waltzing onto the set, McKayla and Brad still putzing with her hair and makeup. They stop before they come all the way in the room, away from the rest of the guys but near enough to me that I can hear every word.

"You look like shit, girl," McKayla is complaining at Emily but scowling at Brad. "Brad, you gotta learn to cover up those dark circles or Meredith is gonna hire a competent makeup artist who can."

Brad scowls. "I'm doing the best I can with Cinder-fucking-ella over here . . . out past curfew. What are you doing with this rat's nest for hair? Meredith said a poufy ponytail and that ain't it!"

I laugh a little, trying to keep it down because their banter makes it sound like Emily looks awful, when the truth is, she looks gorgeous. Yeah, maybe she looks a little bit tired, but I know the reason for that. And it's a damn good reason too.

Before Emily can reply to their antics, Meredith blows onto set like a tornado, Nate following behind, as always, with his goddamn clipboard.

"All right, people," Meredith says loudly, looking around the room at the remaining men, some whose nervousness is showing on their faces like an open book. "We've got a card ceremony first. Two of you will be cut," she announces casually as if reading something off the menu and not potentially crushing a man's dream. "After that, we're on location for sailing today, photo shoots, and short solo dates with each. We'll do some confessional shots onboard, and then a late night for you, Emily, as we've got some filming when we get back." She claps her hands together with finality. "Busy day, everyone. Let's roll!"

As she shouts orders to the camera crew, we start lining up with our cards in our hands. I'm not nervous at all as the dramatic music and ceremony begins. I know there's no way Emily won't match me. Not after everything we shared.

My confidence proves to be spot on. Emily ends up cutting

Carlos and Matt. As much as I want my competition elimi-
nated, I'm sad to see those two go. I would have much rather
she sent Lee packing.

I watch as Emily gives them each a hug and a soft peck on
the cheek before sending them home. Matt actually looks a
little crushed, but he takes it like a man and gives her a smile
of thanks as he is sent off. The smug smirk on Lee's face as
he does causes me to look away. I can't fucking wait until it's
his turn.

I should have warned her about him, I think to myself. But as
soon as I saw her, anything I'd planned to say was driven
from my brain.

After the ceremony, we all get shuttled into SUVs and head
for the marina. Once there, we board a huge, sleek sailboat
and are sent down to our cabins immediately for the crew to
set up on the deck.

I'm in my cabin for all of five minutes before I consider
sneaking out to see Emily. The only thing holding me back is
I'm not sure what today's timeline looks like and don't want
either of us to get caught.

For the next hour, I pace restlessly, thinking about my game
plan until Nate finally shows up, instructing me to come up
on deck.

Up top, my breath catches in my throat as I see Emily almost
immediately. She's lying on a patterned towel on the deck in
a bikini, looking like a goddess basking in the sun, her skin
glistening with a light sheen of oil.

"Hayden," says Meredith, who never seems to be more than a
few feet away, no matter where we are, "this should be easy
for you. I need some shots of you and Emily together. Lovey-

dovey private moment look, maybe some fun in the sun shots too. Once we get all the shots we need, you'll have about thirty minutes to chat below deck while we reset up here for the next suitor. Any questions?"

This is the best news I've heard all day. For once, I don't want someone to strangle Meredith. I can't contain my grin as I shake my head. "No, ma'am." I'm talking to Meredith, but my eyes never leave Emily's. She's so damn enchanting. This is going to be fun.

As I move toward her, I can already feel air crackling between us. Somewhere, I hear Meredith yell, "Action!" but I'm already in the zone.

I lean over Emily, almost in a high push-up position, caging her in with my arms. Feeling desire boil my blood, I growl deeply. "Arch your back for me, Emily. Press your tits up toward me." I give her a wink. "Just play along."

She flushes slightly but does as I ask.

I pause for a moment for the photographer, then drop down to one elbow, bringing the other hand to her face and staring deep into her eyes. I hear the *click* of the camera.

I trace a fingertip down her cleavage, following it with my eyes. *Click.*

She brings a hand up toward my face, and I lean into it, closing my eyes at her touch. *Click.*

I turn my face, catching her index finger in my mouth. *Click.*

I let her finger go with a pop, pressing back to rest on my knees and pulling her up to do the same. Bodies flush to each other, just a breath between us from shoulder to knees, I wrap her ponytail in my hand, pulling her head back a little and meeting her lips in a soft kiss. *Click.* The kiss might be soft, but I'm damn sure not, and I can't help but press our bodies together, grinding my cock against her belly slightly for some relief.

I hear the photographer clear his throat. "Maybe some playful ones now."

I grin and stand, scooping her up into my arms, hoping he's ready to catch her look of surprise. *Click.*

Getting closer to the edge, but not too close, I act like I'm going to throw her into the water. She shrieks and squirms, but I've got a good hold on her and she's not going anywhere. *Click.*

I let her slide down my body, grins on both of our faces. *Click.*

I let out a whoop, picking her up and throwing her over my shoulder and turning so the photographer can catch her upside down smile. *Click.*

Nodding his head, the photographer lets us know he's gotten all he needs.

As if on cue, Meredith appears at our side, grinning from ear to ear. "Bravo, you two. I knew you'd nail it. We definitely got what we needed." She shakes her head. "The viewers are going to need some ice after they see those images. But enough with that, off you go below deck so we can reset."

I grab Emily's hand and start leading her away, but I feel eyes on me and turn around, catching Meredith giving me an appraising look. I know I'm not overstepping boundaries by taking the lead with Emily, so I can't help but wonder what she's thinking. After a moment, I shrug and we continue on, settling in on a white leather couch below deck in a private room. Emily's sitting next to me with my arm around her shoulder. It feels natural, easy.

Emily starts shaking her head, looking at me with wide eyes. "Holy shit, Hayden, that was fucking awesome! If those pics turn out half as hot as they felt, they're gonna use those for all the promos."

I smile. "If only every shoot were as easy as that. I was just doing what I felt with you. You're lucky the photographer interrupted when he did. I was in a zone. Who knows what the fuck I would've done?"

Emily swallows. "What . . . would you have done?" I move toward her, holding steady a breath away for a beat, then taking her mouth with a searing kiss. My hands slip and slide over her skin until I need more and pull her to straddle me. I tease her rigid nipples through her swim top, wanting desperately to slip it to the side. And then I remember.

Shit . . . we're alone, but there are probably cameras here somewhere.

I groan and put my mouth by her ear. "If we were alone, I'd bury myself inside you again right now."

She tenses, realizing what I'm saying about hidden cameras in an instant, and blushes furiously. "I forgot . . . you make me forget."

"Me too," I say. "Come here." I pull her to me, and she rests her head on my shoulder as I curl a tendril of her hair around my finger mindlessly. "Hey, do you have any tattoos?"

Emily looks at me. "Whiplash subject change much? But no, although I've thought about getting an Alice tattoo. You know, from Alice in Wonderland."

I snort a laugh. "Alice in Wonderland?"

Emily shrugs. "I don't know. For some reason, she just resonates for me, a bit of a lost outsider in a confusing world but enjoying the trip, and ultimately, standing up for herself. It's one of my favorite stories."

I stare at her. "That's really telling. You don't really seem like an outsider, but Alice must click for you somehow. Are we in your wonderland trip right now, because I'll admit this whole show thing is a little crazy."

Emily smiles faintly. "Maybe so. I just hope I can stand up to the Queen of Hearts."

I nudge her softly, gently giving her arm a little squeeze. "I think you're the queen of my heart—oh, but let's not do the 'off with his head' part, all right?"

Emily blushes and laughs at the same time. I can't help it. I start going in for another kiss, hidden cameras be damned.

At that exact moment, the door swings opens, and I swear I'm ready to turn into Michael Myers as Meredith pops her head in. "Ooh, looking mighty cozy in here." She grins, her eyes looking us up and down. "But Emily, everything's ready and you're back on deck for photos with Cody . . . make sure he picks you up for some shots to highlight his size and strength."

Emily looks like she's about ready to shove Meredith off the boat herself, but she does as ordered before Meredith turns her attention to me. "And Hayden. You're off to confessional." She claps her hands as I hold in a groan. I want to argue, but I know it'll do no good.

"Let's roll."

Confessional

"*How's it feel to be in the final four?*"

I run my hands through my hair as I look into the camera. "Well, it feels like . . . there's just Emily and me, and sometimes, she gets pulled away to hang out with the other guys. But it's really us. I think we're a done deal and I'm just ready to be done with the show so we can go on from here."

I know it sounds crazy and I've seen people say this on shows before. I never believed it for a second, but I really feel we have a connection, and maybe we've even fallen for each other. We're definitely a match. I can't believe we found each other like this, but we did.

CHAPTER 17

EMILY

"*W*hoa, don't drop me!" I half scream, half giggle as Cody tosses me into the air while the cameraman zips around us, snapping dozens of pictures. After a short 'reset' and some personal time that's supposedly 'private', I'm continuing my photoshoots with the rest of my suitors and trying to seem upbeat and open with each and every one, though it's hard when my mind is on one, in particular.

There's just something about Hayden that . . .

"Chill, I got you," Cody assures me, cradling me in his arms and pulling me against his broad chest. "You're as light as a feather."

"Tell that to my stomach," I reply, smiling as the camera flashes in my eyes. "It was about to empty all over you, tossing me around like that."

Cody chuckles, wiggling his eyebrows at me. "Kinky. I can dig it."

"Gross!" I laugh.

We do several more shots, changing positions, one with me sitting on his shoulders, another riding him piggyback, to show Cody's size and strength like Meredith insisted. For the last shot, he even goes as far as holding me up with one hand, and I swear my side is going to be bruised from all of my weight being centered on his palm.

"That was great, Cody!" Meredith calls, sticking her thumb up and pointing to the stairs. "You two can head below deck while we reset for the next shoot."

We slip down to the same couch I was sitting on with Hayden just minutes ago, and it'd feel strange but the vibe with Cody is just so different. He's almost brotherly with me, teasing and joking, which makes me laugh as I relax beside him.

After a few minutes, Nate comes in, his eyes locked on his clipboard. "Meredith is ready for you again. She said to tell you to stop and see McKayla and Brad for any touchups and be on set in ten minutes."

I nod and look over at Cody, who gives me a smirk. He gives me a quick hug before heading off to do . . . well, whatever the guys are doing when I'm not around. You'd think that being on a boat would mean I'd know everything, but we're on a big boat, bitch. They must have some cabin in the back with video games and fishing rods or something, because the crew seems to bring them from nowhere and they disappear just as quickly.

I hop in a chair in front of McKayla for a quick primp of my hair as Brad simultaneously sweeps powder across the shiny areas. With a flick, McKayla unties my suit and helps me into the next one. I swear, I never thought I'd be comfortable being naked in front of them for wardrobe changes, but the pace is just too rushed for me to be shy. With a minute to spare, I step back on deck.

"Are you all right?" asks Dean when it's his turn, stepping up as I rub my side. He looks handsome, white dress shirt open at the top and the sleeves rolled up, his hair gelled to perfection, but I don't get any butterflies in my stomach like I do with Hayden. "You look like you're holding your ribs."

Don't get me wrong, Dean is handsome in an old Hollywood type of way with his tall, slim physique, brown hair, and crystal clear blue eyes, but I just don't feel a connection with him. I guess it's just one of those things where despite Dean's being near perfect, he just isn't perfect for me.

I flash him a friendly smile. "I'm fine. Now that the Goliath is gone," I say jokingly.

Dean chuckles, flashing his perfect white teeth. "Cody is quite a brute, isn't he?"

I nod. "I'm not sure *brute* is how I'd describe him, but he is a giant. I think he chose the wrong show. He should've been on the Deathmatch version of *Survivor*."

Dean laughs, interlocking my arm with his, turning to face the camera with his dazzling smile. "Or *The Ultimate Fighter*. Something tells me he'd be the last man standing."

"The show's going pretty well," Dean says as we change poses and the lights flash in our eyes. "I'm surprised, actually. When I signed up, I thought this would be one of those things that fell apart within the first week due to booze and scandal. Thirty guys and one chick? Even a sixth grader could see how that would be a recipe for disaster."

"It is," I say, feeling guilty as I think about the stolen

moments with Hayden. "I just hope I have enough personality to make it worth watching."

"I wouldn't worry," Dean soothes. "Trust me, you have more than enough spunk to keep viewers tuning in to watch you break hearts."

"Don't remind me." I've tried very hard not to think about the men I sent home, even though most of them were probably just here for a chance at a quick fifteen minutes of fame.

Dean nods as he places his hand on my hip as the photographer orders him to turn around. "I know, hard to choose and gauge someone from so little time. But hey, I have to say I'm honored to be in the final four, and I'm looking forward to spending even more time with you."

I feel uneasy as I force a grin. "I am too."

I finish out the photo shoot with Dean, enjoying several giggly moments and even a soft, chaste kiss. We finish up out on the extreme front of the boat for a quick posed Titanic-inspired shot with me flinging my arms wide open. When the photographer calls it a wrap, we have alone time to ourselves high above the water instead of disappearing below deck like I did with Hayden and Cody.

"That was great," Dean says, helping me to sit down on the smooth decking.

I nod, smiling. "It was. I'm sure the pictures will turn out fantastic, too."

Dean sits down beside me, taking my hand in his and tracing my fingers with his fingertips. "Not as fantastic as you. You know, I've been looking forward to having a little alone time with you since this deal started. It's even better than I thought it would be."

It breaks my heart, staring into his sky blue eyes and seeing something reflected there but knowing that I'm unable to reciprocate. "Thank you," I say softly, lowering my lashes and staring at my toes.

"Hey, look!" Dean says excitedly. I look up and see him pointing out over the water. "There's a pod of dolphins."

I try to follow his finger's path, but all I see is gorgeous sparkling water for miles in front of us to the horizon. "Where?"

He leans in close, his head just behind my shoulder and his breath on my cheek as he lines up our sight. He points again. "Right there." And suddenly, I see them! A whole group of dolphins, and like it was planned, they begin leaping in the air, their acrobatics amazing to watch. I glance back at Dean excitedly, and he's not looking at their joyous antics but is staring at me, watching me enjoy the moment. He glances at my lips and then moves in for a soft kiss. It's sweet and nice, but there's no heat, and I know he felt the void too when he pulls back, a thoughtful look on his face.

From below, I hear Meredith yell, "Okay, Emily, time to get ready for the last shoot."

Dean helps me stand but puts a stalling hand on my arm. "Hey, Emily? What do you think of Lee?" I glance below to the set, where McKayla and Brad are working on Lee for the photoshoot.

"I'm not certain. He's got a lot going for him," I say, wondering where this is going. "Why do you ask?"

For a moment, it looks like Dean isn't going to say anything and I wonder if he's just looking for gossip to take back to the guys. He finally sighs and speaks up. "It's just that sometimes, you have to be careful about the snakes in the grass. They're camouflaged for a reason."

I frown. "What do you mean by that?"

Before he can answer, Brad and McKayla finish with Lee and he comes over with a swagger, climbing up on the deck with us and giving Dean a polite nod.

"How's it going, Doll?" Lee asks as Dean steps away, leaving me confused. Unlike the other two, I have to admit I am a bit attracted to him.

"Fine now that you're here," I say, flashing a smile that I hope hides the uneasiness I feel from Dean's words.

Lee grins at my compliment, moving in close. I'm enveloped by the smell of his cologne, a spicy fragrance that gives me a heady sensation. "Did they bore you?"

"Not really. We had fun," I say diplomatically. "Just like I hope we'll do."

Lee squares his shoulders, rolling his neck before adjusting his tux. "Well, then, I have to make sure I don't disappoint. Let's own this photoshoot."

After a quick visit with the dynamic duo, I'm shooting with Lee. He keeps me entertained, making me laugh with his banter as we change poses for the photographer. I find myself enjoying his company so much that I forget about Dean's ominous warning and lose track of time.

I feel slightly disappointed when Meredith calls, "That was great, Lee! You're done. You guys can go back below deck for your solo time. Nate will tell you when it's been the allotted thirty minutes, but we'll be here for a while getting everything cleaned up before we head back."

I look at Lee, and he smiles "After you." We head below deck and sit, simply staring out the huge wall of windows as the sun dips down to touch the waves at the horizon line. It's a beautiful moment made even sweeter with Lee's smooth talking. "That's my new number-one sunset. Right here with you." My heart swells. We talk a little more, his attention never wavering from me as we discuss everything and nothing. I'm surprised when I hear Nate calling that it's time to head back.

*A*fter the crew is packed up, they join us for the rest of the ride back to the mansion. I spend a lot of my time on the ride back watching the guys interact and absorbed in my thoughts. I'm dreading doing the confessional Meredith wants me to do, exhausted from spending a day out on the water. But I know I have no choice.

We pull up to the mansion, and after I say my goodbyes to Cody, Dean, and Lee, Hayden gives me a little wink. I don't have time to wonder what the wink is about as McKayla and Brad swarm me as soon as I get out of the SUV.

"Come on, chica," McKayla says. "Let's do a quick touch-up for hair and makeup before your confessional. We've already grabbed your wardrobe."

Brad purses his lips, looking at my face with a critical eye. "I think I can tweak what's already here and not start from scratch, save us some time."

McKayla snaps her fingers. "Ooh, good thinking. I'll do an updo and let a few of these salty waves trail down by your face." She nods, looking at me as if she can see the vision right in front of her face. "Yup. Uh-huh. Perfection!"

"Damn, is the earth about to end?" I joke as the two give each other a high-five and get to work. "I think this is the nicest you two have ever been to each other."

"Bitch!" Brad snaps at McKayla, showing that I spoke too soon as they swirl around each other, getting me ready. "Get out the way! You're in my light. Scoot that prissy ass over or Em is gonna have stripes for contour."

McKayla stops twirling a curl of mine to scowl at Brad like he's roadkill. "Not my fault you can't do makeup for shit." She adds some more curls to my hair before stopping to eye it critically, turning to Brad for his opinion. "What do you think? Too poufy?"

Brad finishes applying blush to my cheeks and sneers at my head. "Do you even know the meaning of the phrase *too much volume*, Ms. Bouffant Betty? Any more air in there and she's gonna float away on the next stiff breeze."

I let out a laugh. The sound of my giggles seems to remind McKayla of something because she says, "Oh, and Ms. Thing, I got a secret message for you from your honey buns."

I stare at her, my heart thumping in my chest as she teases it out until I'm nearly ready to explode. I might have spent most of the day with three other men, but honestly, I've been comparing them to Hayden. "Come on! What?"

McKayla makes a face and relents with a smirk. "Third floor, fifth door on the right. Midnight. Apparently, you sleep-walk . . . a lot."

Brad chuckles at the look on my face. "Just don't get caught, girl. It's so against the rules. I know we got on your case before, but I ain't ever been a basic bitch, so I suggest you go get you some of that fine piece or I'll have to show up at midnight myself."

I laugh. "Sorry, Brad, don't think Hayden swings that way."

Brad raises an eyebrow. "Honey, you trying to tell me something? Big enough to swing? Good to know, good to fucking know. And if I were you . . . I'd wear something thin and clingy."

Five minutes later, I'm sitting in front of a green screen in a white t-shirt, Nate explaining that they can edit it later so that the colors look flattering on my skin. Whatever. I'm ready to roll, as Meredith would say.

Speak of the devil, and here she is.

"All right, Emily," Meredith says, giving me a serious look. "I need a lot out of you tonight. I need a full breakdown of each guy . . . all his good traits that make you like him and all his not-so good traits that make him not the one. I need details, with examples as much as possible. We'll use these snippets to go back with footage from the dates, so when you talk about Cody helping you bungee jump, it'll flash to that scene. Got it?"

"I got it, but I don't really have anything bad to say about any of them, honestly," I say slowly, not wanting to cross Meredith but at the same time not just wanting to search my memory of things to nitpick. "Won't that make me seem petty?"

Meredith rolls her eyes. "Look, not every guy is your match. Everyone knows that, including them, so I need some footage of what might make them a match and what might not. It's not personal. It's just how the game works. Trust me, they're confessing their thoughts on the dates too."

Her words give me pause. I just hadn't thought about them all sitting around and talking about me with each other, on and off camera. It makes me slightly uncomfortable, and I'm more than a little curious about what they've said about me.

With those troubling thoughts running through my head, I film for over an hour, doing snippets about each suitor, recalling moments with them and what I felt and thought at the time. It actually helps me focus and process a little as Meredith asks me leading questions, getting me to talk more than I'd planned on initially. At the end, Meredith and I go through the procedure for the card matches the next day. After spending the day with all four men, my choices on who stays and who goes is a no-brainer.

Meredith even agrees that Dean and Cody should go and that Lee and Hayden should stay.

"We've already been showing early scenes to test audiences and those two are the definite favorites," Meredith says. "So I'm not surprised they're your favorites too. Hayden seems a little growly sometimes, but hot enough, I guess. From this side of the camera, you really have sparks with Lee though. When y'all kiss, it's Hollywood magic with little fireworks popping all around you."

I arch an eyebrow in surprise. I've been trying not to seem biased but I would think my true choice would be obvious to anyone watching. "Really? I kinda feel just the opposite. I think I've got a real connection with Hayden. Maybe even a match!" I laugh nervously at my own joke, but Meredith's lips barely tilt into a smile.

"Hmm, I don't know," she says quietly. "Think about it, but I'd pick Lee if I were you." She doesn't say it directly, but it almost feels like he's who she wants the winner to be. With that said, she walks off, Nate trailing behind, her making notes as she spouts off about tomorrow's scenes.

I stare at them walking away for a moment, thinking about what she said, and then remember with a flush that it's gotta be close to midnight and I need to hustle inside for some "sleepwalking".

---

*a*n hour later, I'm closing the fifth door on the third floor behind me in the dark, whispering, "Hayden?"

I breathe a sigh of relief when I hear Hayden's voice. "Right here. I thought you'd never get here. Come here, woman."

He wraps me up in his arms, pulling me in tight to his body as he takes my mouth with a hot kiss. He's ravenous, and I kiss him back just as hard, my body demanding satisfaction. He groans, murmuring, "God, I was so close to coming in my shorts today just from your straddling me, your hot pussy pressing up against my cock."

"You had me the same way," I admit, reaching down and grabbing his ass. "I've been on overload all day because of you."

"Well, that's something I can take care of," Hayden says, moving down and pulling the hem of my sleepshirt up and off, leaving me bare. Taking a nipple into his mouth, he teases me until they're hard and aching before looking up into my eyes. "I wanted to lick these pretty pink nipples, have the taste of your salty skin on my tongue."

We move together, me almost ripping his shirt off so I can be skin to skin with him, our tongues tangling the whole time. I pause the kiss, and he pulls back, looking at me questioningly. With a smirk, I drop to my knees. "I want your taste on my tongue too. You going to let me suck you?"

Hayden groans, running his hand through my hair and grabbing a fistful as he looks at me in wonder. "Fuck, Em. I might come just from your words and how fucking good you look on your knees in front of my cock."

Hearing no argument, I pull his shorts and boxer briefs down, sitting back on my heels for a moment to take him in, seeing him bathed in silvery moonlight. He's beautiful. "Wow," I murmur, and even without looking up, I know he's smiling. I move in, licking and kissing and sucking his cock down my throat as he fists my hair. He's holding back, letting me have control but showing me the pace he wants. I oblige, but suddenly, he pulls his hips back. I pout, licking my lips as I look up at him. "I wasn't done . . ."

"You have me so fucking horny I'm about to come, and while I'd love to come deep down your throat, I want your pussy tonight." Pulling me to my feet, he turns me, and I bend over a nearby table, thrusting my ass out toward him. "Call me a liar if that isn't the sexiest thing I've ever seen."

"Liar," I tease, looking over my shoulder, "because *you* are the sexiest thing I've ever seen."

Hayden slides behind me, pulling my body to him as he caresses me with his hands, the hot, heavy thickness of his cock pressing against my ass. Reaching around, his right hand cups my breast, kneading and pulling on my nipple while his other hand cups my pussy, rubbing and sliding his fingers between my lips until I'm trembling. Hayden rains kisses on my neck and shoulders, my skin burning with his passion, and I reach back, grabbing his hair and turning to kiss him hard. Hayden slips two fingers inside me, but it's not enough, and I break our kiss, shaking my head and letting him know what I need by bending over more.

He slips a condom over his cock, giving me a light smack to my ass cheek as he lines up with my pussy. "You ready for me?" he asks, running the tip of his cock through my slippery folds.

He can damn well feel that I'm more than ready, so I just groan, barely choking out, "Hayden. Please." And he fills me with one deep, almost savage thrust, bottoming out balls deep, and we both cry out, needing a moment to adjust. He holds my hips steady, slowly starting to move in and out, both of us panting.

After the almost feral nature of his first thrust and the fiery harshness of everything leading up to this, I'm shocked as Hayden seems to take his time, his strokes not hard but still fast, the lack of impact startling and electric. I'm caught, nothing but pleasure shaking my body from top to bottom. I squeeze him, desperate to make him feel as good as what he's doing to me, and Hayden moans, encouraging me.

Faster than either of us would like, we're falling off the edge together, muffling our cries as Hayden kisses my neck. He covers my mouth with his hand, and I totally give in, shaking as he holds me close. He pulls out to turn me around and wraps his arms around me to carry me to a couch.

We sit next to the window, my head nestled on his chest, watching the beautiful lights from the city below us. Suddenly curious, I look around. "What is this room?"

Hayden glances around, humming. "Seems to be storage for now. I guess they had to move furniture around downstairs for filming?"

"Filming . . . this is so strange. I still can't believe I'm on a fucking love connection game show. And that I might've actually met a love connection . . ." Shit, I didn't mean to say it like that. Right now, it's just lust, but maybe . . . I glance up at Hayden, expecting him to be shocked or horrified or laughing at me.

Instead, he has a bright smile on his face, truly looking happy. "Me either, and I don't know what comes after all of this, but I know that I want to figure it out with you." He pulls me closer, and I nestle against him, knowing that we'll have to go back to our rooms soon . . . but not yet.

CHAPTER 18

"Cody, I'm sorry, but we're not a match."

I swallow, knowing that means another one of the 'good guys' is gone. Damn, we'd just had a pleasant breakfast too, sitting around and enjoying a gourmet spread. The camera crew got in the way a little, but it was fun to chill with the guys. Cody and Dean, at least. It sucks that just minutes later, just as the sun's really coming up and most people would be getting ready to go to work, Emily has cut another, and it wasn't Lee. But that's the way it is, and I knew as soon as Meredith came storming onto the patio what was up.

"Will Hayden and Dean please come forward?" Emily asks, and I take a moment. With today's cut, Meredith decided to do it in twos. Lee and Cody were up first, flipping their cards along with Emily. Cody took his loss well, shaking hands with me and Dean before giving Emily a hug.

Lee, of course, looks cocky as fuck as Dean and I step

forward. He doesn't have anything to worry about now. And in his mind, this show is already wrapped up.

Dean and I stand side by side, but before Emily can start her lines about the cards, Dean steps forward. "Dean?" Emily asks, confused.

I can see it in his eyes. He knows he's been cut. I'd be stupid to say I don't agree with him, and it hits me right in the gut to know that a guy I consider a friend is going to lose. But it's me or him. There's more than that in Dean's eyes, though, as he looks back at me, then at Emily.

"Emily, I have a pretty good idea what's under my card," he says, waving his hand when Meredith goes to protest. "But for the past few days, I've had fun here. I thought, when I came here, that I'd hate everyone. Hell, I figured we'd be at each other's throats and ready to fight over you."

"I heard that," Cody, who's walked off set but is still next to Joe the cameraman, says.

"But as the competition continued, I found that not only have I enjoyed each and every second that I've gotten to spend with you, but I've also met a few guys who, back home, I wouldn't mind sharing a beer with and calling my friends. That includes you, Hayden."

"Bro," I whisper, and Dean turns to me.

"If I'm wrong, and I'm just talking out of my ass and you're the one cut while I go on, it still doesn't change the fact that I've made a good friend."

"You too," I agree. "For damn sure, we're gonna stay in touch after this. No matter what."

Dean offers me his hand, and I shake before getting pulled into a bro hug with him. He pats me on the shoulder, and I can tell by the look in his eyes that he's got something on his mind.

He turns back to Emily and clears his throat. "Emily, regardless of what's under my card, I think you're a beautiful woman. The sort of woman who deserves happiness. So no matter what, choose wisely. Think about who's going to be there for you, who's going to try and be someone real . . . and who's just here to get a little bit of publicity and his fifteen minutes of fame."

Emily looks shaken, and I can tell Meredith isn't liking this. According to the contracts we signed, we're not allowed to directly talk shit about the other contestants to Emily, so it's likely no one has told her what a fake fucking douchebag Lee is. But Dean just damn-near stomped on that contract, and while I'm glad for Emily to get a bit of the truth, I hope it doesn't put Dean in a bad spot with the producers. As it is, the editors are going to have a hell of a time chipping that up for the audience.

Finally, Emily speaks, though she still looks confused. "Thank you, Dean."

Knowing that anything I want to say would just pile on with Dean's comments, I simply give Emily a nod, hoping she understands, and step forward next to Dean.

Fifteen seconds later, seeing the match on my card, I'm torn. Of course, most of me is happy, but there's a shadow inside that says it's not fair that Lee is here and Dean's not. If she knew who he really was, he would've been gone a long time ago. But I shake Dean's hand one more time for the cameras, and he whispers in my ear, "Take that fucking snake down, okay? For Emily's sake, even if you two aren't long-term material."

"You can count on it," I promise him. Dean turns and gives Emily a hug and kiss on the cheek, then walks off set. Meredith gives it a few seconds for the cameras to get their departing shots before clapping her hands again. I swear she treats us like a class of kindergarteners.

"All right, people . . . last two standing. You know what that means." She waggles her eyebrows at us. We all stare blankly, not knowing what she's talking about. Meredith sighs. Maybe we are kindergarteners to her. "Fantasy suite dates!"

She says it like we're supposed to start jumping around in excitement. A crew member sets up the spinning wheel and button for Emily to push, and as the cameras roll, locations start to scroll across the screen. Obviously, by now, we know that the destination is already set up and the button push is just for show. But the flashing cities do build excitement. Emily plays it up, yelling cheerfully. "No whammies!" as she presses the button and the screen stops on . . . Las Vegas!

It's hard not to smile at that, each of us hollering, "Vegas, Baby!" on cue. Everyone is excited, even the crew, for a trip away, it seems. A night in a fantasy suite with Emily sounds pretty fucking sweet too . . . I just have to remember the cameras are going to be right in our faces, though, but I'll figure out something. They damn sure can't see under the covers. I glance at Emily, who looks back with a slight blush in her cheeks, and I swear she's thinking the same thing.

Meredith lets the cheers die down before continuing. "Okay, Emily, get packed. Guys, I'd like to have meetings with each of you in the office."

We follow Meredith and Nate to the front of the house, and

Lee goes in first with them while I hang in a chair in the hall-way. I keep hoping to get a glance of Emily, but no dice, although Cody comes by with his bags over his shoulder. He gives me a nod and a little salute, his broad shoulders unbowed by getting cut. Fifteen minutes after that, Lee walks out with a big-ass grin from ear to ear and it's my turn. I close the door behind me, sitting down in a chair next to Meredith, Nate behind the desk clicking on the laptop and ignoring us.

"So Hayden, how do you think this is all going? What's your take on everything?" Meredith asks, sitting in her chair like queen of the fucking world.

"Uh, it seems to be going great. Emily and I have hit it off, and I think she's gonna pick me."

Meredith looks a bit shocked, but it seems forced somehow, then she switches to a pitying look, picking up a tablet computer and tapping at it. "Look, Hayden. This is all smoke and mirrors, a setup, if you will, much like your photography work. I'm sure you understand. Here's the deal . . . you seem like such a great guy. In fact, we've done some test screening with preview audiences and they love you. A lot. But I'm afraid you're getting a little lost in the magic here."

I'm confused by what she's saying, although the test audi-ences liking me sounds like a good thing, right? "You lost me. What are you saying?"

Meredith hands her tablet to Nate, who runs off like the good little minion that he is before coming back and going back to work with his computer. "Well, here's the thing. We knew a while back that Emily is going to match with Lee. She's practically said as much in her confessionals, although she does say sweet things about you too."

"Practically?" I ask, raising an eyebrow. "Somehow, I doubt that."

Meredith shakes her head, and I can tell she's trying to talk her way around something difficult. "Listen, there's just so much chemistry between them. The test audiences are saying Lee's the betting man's favorite. And . . . " She pauses, but I can't say anything as my mind is racing. *Chemistry with Lee? She's picking him? What the fuck?*

Seeing my expression, Meredith continues. "Well, that's not important right now. Hayden, the thing is, you test so well with the preview audiences, so we have an idea. It'll get you lots of continued exposure that'd be great for your career. Your agent already said you'd be interested."

I blink, still feeling like I've been punched in the gut with a large padded fist. "Jay? You talked to Jay? About what?"

Meredith smiles, and while it looks friendly, I can't help but think she looks a little predatory. "Matchmaker, Season Two . . . it's you." I look at her blankly, obviously not the reaction she expected. She waves her hand, as if trying to conjure magic or something. "You'll be the runner-up when Emily and Lee match, and then you'll be the star of next season with a cast of ladies trying to match with you. It's brilliant, if I do say so myself, if a bit used. But like they say, if it isn't broke, don't fix it. I'll need a bit of confessional about you two being hot but maybe not all it seems, and probably a bit of on-screen coolness. Nothing major, just help make it obvious you two aren't relationship material so you don't have rebound baggage for Season Two coverage. We want you to be likeable still, just not the fairytale prince . . . of this season, anyway."

She's rambling, talking like this is a done deal, but I don't know what to think . . . I'm still stuck on Emily and Lee. I clear my throat until I get her attention. "Uh, that sounds interesting . . . but I think I've got a shot with Emily still. I could still be her Match."

Meredith tsks at me, obviously getting frustrated. "Romantic till the end, huh? So dreamy . . . the girls are gonna eat that shit up. Look, you've got a contract to take direction, follow a script as needed, and I'm not throwing you under the bus here. I'm offering you something bigger, a shot at your dream. I need you to get on board here or you could jeopardize what we've got planned."

I shake my head. There's contracts, and then there's the right damn thing to do. "Even if she picks Lee, and I don't think she will, I'm not saying shitty things about Emily because of it."

Meredith gives me a look of almost pitying compassion and turns to Nate. "Nate . . . can you roll the scenes of Lee and Emily yesterday, please?" She looks at me, her eyes soulfully sad. "Sorry, but sometimes, it's easier if you just see it with your own eyes."

Nate turns his laptop around, and I see Emily and Lee joking around during their photo shoot. She's smiling and laughing at him as he grabs her around the waist, whispering in her ear, but the mic doesn't catch what he says. Nate fast-forwards to the hidden camera footage in the cabin of the yacht. I knew there were cameras, those sneaky fucks! My gratification at being right is immediately squashed when I see Lee and Emily basically making out. He's kissing her, pressing her back to the couch, and her hands are pressed to his chest. I look up at Meredith, shocked at what I'm seeing. Nate is going to let it play, but Meredith gives him a cutting off gesture.

"As I said, it's quite something to see them together. I'm sorry you weren't expecting that."

With one more fast-forward, Emily fills the screen in a confessional. "Lee is so intense, he overwhelms me with his passion and I just get so lost . . ." Nate clicks again, and a new video springs up. "Hayden is the kind guy you fantasize about, an exciting rule-breaker. He scares me a bit because I think he could break my heart without even trying." She lets out a little laugh. "He probably leaves a trail of broken-hearted girls begging for more wherever he goes."

The screen goes black again, and Meredith turns back to me. "I'm sorry to blindside you this way. But really, this is for the best. Think of it this way. It'll be a great move for your career. And maybe you'll meet your real match next season! I'll draw up the papers and send them to your agent." Defeated, I simply drop my head, my agreement stuck in my throat.

Confessional

"*So we're off to Vegas for fantasy suite dates. Not sure of my odds with Emily at this point, but 50/50 sounds pretty good, I guess. She's a sweet girl . . . just hope she's happy with whoever she picks.*"

Off camera, Meredith waves her hands, scribbling on a white board. I look at her, shrugging my shoulders. What the fuck else does she want? "LOVE" Meredith's written, and my heart clenches in my chest a little as I turn back to the camera.

"Oh, do I love her? That's a really tough question, you know? I mean, love's got a ton of different meanings, and Emily is pretty loveable. But if you mean in love *. . . uh, I don't know if we've had enough time to really fall in love, so no, I don't think I'm in love with her . . . yet."*

God, I hate being a liar.

CHAPTER 19

I spend less than five minutes looking out over the bright lights of Vegas before I turn and give in to my childish impulses, running through the suite I'm in to take a flying flop into the big bed, enjoying its fluffy comfort. It's like landing in a giant pile of feathers, and as I turn over, I throw my arms and legs up while giggling.

After a few moments, I relax back, questions flooding my head. How in the world did I get here? I mean, I know, but at the same time . . . stuff like this doesn't happen to girls like me.

And how am I gonna go on camera and pick a happily ever after? Obviously, I'm leaning toward Hayden, but how do I know? Lee doesn't seem like a bad guy. He's handsome and sexy in his way, but he's just not Hayden, who takes heat to a level I didn't even realize could exist. Lee just can't compete with that.

Before I can think too much, McKayla and Brad barge in, not even bothering to knock. McKayla seems to be in her element in Vegas—big personality, big hair, and full of bad choices. Hell, here she's basically calm and conservative by comparison to most folks. "Hey, Chickadee! Time to get you primped up for your date with Hayden tonight. Not that you need primping for that man. He seems to like you just fine, dirty and in the dark."

I blush, sitting up and trying not to grin guiltily. "Yeah, last night was awesome. We talked for long time, and it seems like I might've actually made a real love connection on this crazy game. I didn't exactly mean it that way, but I accidentally said that last night and he didn't freak out!"

Brad, who's setting up his makeup kit, gives me a surprised look. "Uhm, excuse me . . . did you say you mentioned 'love connection' and he was okay with that? There's only two things that means. He's thinking he might be in love with you too, or he's thinking, 'Oh, shit, I just stuck my dick in crazy. Back away slowly and don't make eye contact.' It's a cardinal rule—don't stick your dick in crazy."

"And if anyone knows about sticking their dicks in crazy, it's Brad's former boyfriends," McKayla adds. I laugh because they're both hilarious, although Brad doesn't seem to be smiling quite so much at the moment.

I can't help but laugh because it's funny as hell, but their comments are kind of freaking me out at the same time. I think back. Did he seem nervous after I said that? I don't think so. We talked about the show, the dates we've been on, and some vague hopes and dreams type stuff. But nothing he said made me think he might be nervous or upset.

As McKayla and Brad hover around me like a pair of overly caffeinated bees, I relive every moment of our date by the pond and in the storage room. More than the sex, which was amazing, I think about everything we shared about families, our lives back home, all the little random tidbits that make me feel like I really know him. I analyze every word, every facial expression that might give me some insight as to Hayden's thoughts about the future.

Future. I pause. He never said anything about us after the show. Is that bad? I can't worry about that now as Nate comes in, ready to escort me out to the living area for a private dinner. Brad smacks him away, chasing him out of the room. "Don't you see that she's hardly dressed for a dinner? Now out! We'll get her dressed, but until then, this room is us bitches only!"

Nate looks like he wants to argue, but Brad's having none of it, closing the door and turning around. "Yass, queen, finally! That boy is so annoying."

"Yeah, well, unless you want the real Queen B in here kicking your skinny ass, let's get our princess here dressed quickly," McKayla says, helping me up. "Wardrobe already delivered your dress for tonight, so strip like you're Supergirl."

I have to admit that the dress is amazing, a deep red piece with a high collar and piping that hugs my curves and leaves me feeling sexier than ever before. Brad gives my lipgloss a final touchup then stands back, admiring his work. "Honey, you look hot enough that they're gonna ban you from Vegas. The desert can't take this much heat!"

"Let's go, let's go!" McKayla urges me, pushing me toward the door before whispering in my ear, "Brad's right. Have fun, babe."

Nate looks flustered but keeps his mouth shut as he escorts me up one floor to the fantasy suite that we'll be using tonight, a glamorous suite that's supposed to have an Asian motif, like my dress, I guess. Stepping in, everything's in shades of green, red, gold, and black, with lots of natural looking lanterns, wood floors, and paper screens to complete the illusion. Hayden stands when I come in the room, pulling my chair out for me and helping me get seated. "You look beautiful," he says as he helps my chair in. "Truly beautiful."

Before I can answer, Meredith interrupts. "Okay, you two. Just chat, romance, just a regular date, and we'll do a kiss shot in front of the doors and then off for the night. Good?" I notice Meredith give Hayden a pointed look, but she yells, "Action!" and I jump into date-mode.

Like our room, our date has an Asian motif, with teppanyaki grilled meat and vegetables served to us with cups of Japanese sake wine. "I kinda wish we'd have done this at a real restaurant," I say as our waiter brings us our third course, rice and vegetables. "I've been to one place, and the chef was as much theater as he was cook."

"I've been to places like that too," Hayden says, chuckling. "Last place I went to, the chefs at the two tables worked together, at one point taking this piece of tiger prawn and, using the big barbecue fork he had, he slung it across the room to his partner, who caught it as a 'taste test'. It was good shrimp, too."

As the wine and delicious food flows, we talk and laugh, but it doesn't feel the same. I swear something is off, and I'm not sure what. Hayden just feels a little distant, like he's got something else on his mind. Numerous times during our conversation, his answers seem hesitant, trailing off when I swear he's still got something to say. Brad's words run through my head, making doubts creep in, and I try to assuage them by asking what he plans for after the show.

"So . . . after all this is over, what's on your calendar for the future?"

I'm hoping he'll say something about us. Instead, Hayden sets down his cup of sake and for the first time looks . . . I don't know, hurt? "I don't know what's after this. I guess I'll check in with my agent and see what offers have come in for me. I'll probably take a trip home to see my mom and dad since I haven't talked to them since this circus started." He smiles, but it doesn't reach his eyes. "What about you?"

"I guess, well, I'd like to go see my friends back home. I know Cassie has to be wondering if I fell off the edge of the earth, and I miss the kids. After that, though, it kinda depends. I mean, couples should try and coordinate their lives, you know? And I'm sure they'll want us to do some sort of publicity for the show."

"Yeah, you're right," Hayden says, letting the conversation drop. Dinner finishes with delicious ginger ice creams, and we move to the bedroom door for the kiss shot. He moves toward me, his eyes fastened to my lips and never meeting mine. It's a good kiss because Hayden is a good kisser, but the fire isn't there. I bite my lip uncertainly, trying to read him, but Meredith interrupts with another one of her yells. "Cut! Off to bed . . . sweet dreams!"

We slip into the bedroom of the suite and it's quiet. Too quiet. I'd been looking forward to being nearly slammed against the wall as Hayden overwhelmed me with kisses. For him to say to hell with it, let any hidden cameras watch as he gave me a complete and thorough fucking until my body is nothing but pleasure-filled jelly.

Instead, Hayden goes over to the dresser and shrugs off his jacket without even looking at me. It's like he doesn't even want to share the same room as me, and my nervousness ratchets up another notch. I cross the room and put a hand on his shoulder, turning to look him in the eye. "Is everything okay? You seem different. Distant."

Hayden won't seem to meet my eyes, and questions start to creep into my brain. What's changed in the past twenty-four hours? Was Brad right? "Everything is fine. I'm just tired, I guess. This is a lot to process." He waves his hands around like he's encompassing everything, and I don't know if he means the show, me, or us. Either way, I'm scared to ask. I know he's lying, but about what, I don't know.

"Well, I think I'll get changed then," I whisper, going over to the dresser where wardrobe said they set up my pajamas. I open up the drawer, and to hell with pajamas. They gave me some 'fuck me' lingerie, a form-fitting cami with matching panties and nothing else. I should feel sexy, primed for seduction and more, but I don't, and when I turn around, I see that Hayden's also changed. He's got on a pair of black silk pajama pants that make him look sexy as hell, but the coldness in his eyes feels like a punch in the stomach.

We climb into bed, awkward at first as we try and keep some space between us until finally, Hayden moves in closer. I adjust until he's the big spoon for my little spoon. I snuggle in, wiggling my ass against him teasingly, but he just pulls me tighter, not letting me move. He absently twirls a finger through my curls, wrapping and unwrapping them around his finger. We lie there, the wine and the silence making my body relax until we're almost asleep and I can't stand it anymore. "Hayden, I really care about you."

He replies in a voice that's barely above a whisper. "I know . . . and it's okay."

Before I can ask what the hell he means, I hear him start to softly snore. I want to turn over, to wake him up, but I can't find the strength to do it. Instead, I lie in the dark, my brain buzzing and swirling with questions.

What was that?

What does that mean?

Is he backing off from me, from us?

Does he understand that I want to tell him the truth, that I want to tell him that he's the one I want, but that I can't, simply because I don't know if we're being bugged even now? That I want to crawl in his lap and cover his face with kisses? That the only thing stopping me is that I don't want to throw everyone under the bus who has put so much work into this show?

My mind whirling, I think I'll never sleep, but held tight in Hayden's arms, I drift off dreaming of him. It's a beautiful dream, the two of us in a house a lot like the ones back home, comfortable and cozy. There's me and Hayden, and my belly is huge with our baby, a little girl that we've already decided to name Laetitia. It's a wonderful dream, even if I'm not too sure where the name comes from.

The next day starts too early, with Nate waking us up and herding us out of the room. I get a chance to look over at Hayden as he pulls a t-shirt and some exercise shorts on, but I can't say what's on my mind with Nate buzzing around and practically shoving me out the door. "You're to spend the day by yourself," he says as I spare a last glance at Hayden, who's looking at me with what I swear is heartbreak in his eyes. "Meredith and the producers thought that would give you the best chance to make a decision without being influenced one way or another. We've got a few solo scenes scheduled, a little blackjack at the tables, some contemplative shots over-looking the Strip and stuff like that, and interviews, too, you'll be—"

"What are the guys going to do?"

"Hayden's going to have a confessional scene to do, and then we'll be taking him around for his setup shots. You won't be in the same locations, though, and Lee's already out doing his thing. Just think of it this way—it'll let you build the antici-pation for your dinner and overnight with Lee."

Nate keeps buzzing, but I'm not really listening. All I know is that something's wrong between me and Hayden, and I won't have a chance to talk with him before my date with Lee. At this point, I don't even want to go through with it. I don't know what's going on with Hayden, but I don't want to pick Lee when my heart is somewhere else.

CHAPTER 20

EMILY

Confessional

"*My fantasy suite date with Hayden was a little unexpected. He seemed a bit distracted but still a gentleman. Of course, we laughed. It's easy to laugh with Hayden, and the food was delicious. It was just that I always felt like there was this . . . distance. You know, like the bamboo screens that surrounded us, how they have the sheer screens where you can see the outline of whatever's on the other side, but it's not clear. That's kinda how it felt, like it was us, but not as vibrant as before.*"

I take a deep breath, biting my lip as I read the comment Meredith writes on her whiteboard, THE BEDROOM? "*Well, afterward, of course, we spent the night together, and Hayden is . . . he's probably one of the best snugglers on the planet. He held me in his arms all night and it felt good to be surrounded by his warmth. I think maybe I'm just reading too much into my worries, because it felt so good to be in his arms. Hayden's got the kind of arms that you just know are going to be there for you and protect you for as long as you're with him.*"

"Okay, that's good. Cut," Meredith says. "Emily, before you head out today for the rest of your shots, I'd like to have a chat with you in the living room. Nate, chase all the vampires out of there for me. This is off camera, okay?"

"Got it, boss," Nate says, hurrying away. I hear yelling in the next room as McKayla threatens to make Nate her bitch if he talks to her like that again, but within a minute or two, everything is quiet, and Nate comes back. The three of us head into the living room, where I can see that all the cameras, at least temporarily, are turned off.

Meredith takes a seat on one of the chairs while Nate hovers nearby. "Emily, my dear, have a seat. We need to talk through your date."

I scrunch up my eyebrows, confused. "Isn't it the same as last night? Dinner and sleepover on camera, just the theme is supposed to be different?"

Meredith nods, glancing at her perfect gel nails before looking up and giving me a pitying expression. "Well, yes. But I more meant the direction the show is heading. Last night was basically painful to watch. Hayden is a great guy, but he's not pulling through on camera."

The cameras. Always the cameras. I thought that being on reality TV would be fun, but right about now, I want nothing more than to have a baseball bat and five minutes alone with all the cameras. I shake my head, leaning forward and putting my elbows on my knees. "He said he was tired, maybe distracted last night. But our other dates have been better. You even said the photo shoot was great."

Nate inhales audibly, and Meredith cuts her eyes to him. Nate's eyebrows raise as if he's asking Meredith a question, but she shakes her head. I don't know what the silent conversation is about and don't have a chance to ask as Meredith looks back at me. "Test audiences are loving both Hayden and Lee, but there's just something about you and Lee onscreen. It's fireworks and magic. I need to see that on your date."

I knew there were going to be certain elements of the show where the producers would 'advise' me. It was in the contract, and more than once, Meredith has asked me during cuts to save a guy who was on the cusp for one more cut for various reasons. I've always gone along with it because I knew he wouldn't make it in the end, but I assumed the final choice on who wins would be mine. "Uhm, I'm really leaning toward Hayden right now, so I don't want to do anything too over the top. I mean, Lee's a nice guy, and sure, there's a spark with him, but I don't feel the same way about him that I do about Hayden."

The silence stretches out for a long time, Meredith looking at me like I'm stupid while Nate shifts from foot to foot like a little boy who needs to pee in church. Finally, Meredith replies. "This isn't really you picking. This is a whole production team decision that you have a vote in, but ultimately, we're making TV that sells here. And trust me, Lee and you, that's good TV."

"Excuse me?" I ask, stunned. "I was told the choices were mine, especially the final winner. Isn't what you're saying, like, illegal or something? At the very least, it's wrong and misleading."

Meredith ignores me, looking at Nate, who is obviously ready for orders. "Make a note. We've edited Hayden to look good for test audiences, but we'll show some of the less flattering things he's said in confessionals for the later episodes to lead up to Emily choosing Lee."

My jaw drops at her words, and I speak up, getting her attention. "Less flattering things? What are you talking about? What did he say?"

Meredith turns back as Nate pauses his note-taking, obviously eager to be dismissed. She appears to waffle a bit, hesitant. "Hmm, I'm not sure you really want to see those . . ."

The hell I don't, especially if I'm about to pick him on national TV. I don't want to look stupid if he's been playing me. I don't want to be that naïve. God, I can see the headlines on TMZ now, *Matcher's Flame Burns Out Fast!* I don't have the spit in my mouth to say anything, though, and instead look at her with anguished eyes.

Meredith must see my answer on my face. "If you're sure, my dear." She turns to Nate with a smile, "Can you find—"

Nate nods and opens his laptop. With barely a couple of clicks, he has the file queued up and turns the screen toward me.

Hayden pops up on screen. I remember that shirt from one of the earliest days of the show. "*Some of the guys are jerks, just out for their fifteen minutes of fame. Lee is a bit sleazy. Not sure what his endgame is, but I don't think it's Emily.*"

All right, that's not particularly nice, but not so bad. I mean, everyone's got opinions, and it was early on in the show. I don't get what's so bad about that. "And?"

"Are you sure . . .?" Meredith asks, and I nod once more. Nate clicks a few more times, and a different confessional pops up.

"Off to Vegas. 50/50 odds I guess. No, I don't think I'm in love with her."

I gasp, my heart shattering, and Meredith gets up, sitting

down next to me before covering my hands with her own. "I'm so sorry, honey. I didn't know you were that caught up with him. Hard to hear, I know, but at least now you know where you stand. Go cry a few tears, put on your big girl panties, and get ready. You've got a lot of shots to do today. Don't worry, you can have some fun with it. You've got a date with a guy who really likes you and whom you really like too. And that's all that matters."

She's right. I need to cry right now, but I'll rally. I don't have a choice.

***

"So, Emily, how was your day yesterday?" Lee asks me as we sit down in the dining nook of this particular fantasy suite. The theme is European castle, and while to me it's a little more Cinderella castle than real castle, Lee looks handsome in his tuxedo while I feel regal in the full-length fitted gown that I'm wearing.

"It was . . . more difficult than I thought it'd be," I admit, sipping the white wine that's coming with the first course. "How about you?"

Lee smiles softly, and I think for the first time that he looks a little nervous. "To be honest, I spent the whole day racking my brain. You see, I know this is probably the last chance I have to make an impression on you, so this is the time to lay it all out there. I want to make a very good impression."

"I feel that pressure too. It's not just you trying to make a good impression, it's me too. I want to be myself and make the match that feels right, for both of us." Lee understands, and dinner becomes serious, not a laughing feel-good date, but instead, he asks me deep questions about where I see myself in the future.

"So, you really want to see a revolution in education?"

I nod, chewing the lobster medallion that we've been served as our main course. It's delicate and delicious, and if things keep up like this, I'm going to have to skip breakfasts for the next couple of years to make up for all the rich food on this show. "I do. I'd like to see schools with teachers who are able to be inventive and creative with their lessons, not locked in to teaching to the mandated state tests. A place where the community works together to make sure the students are ready to learn, not hungry and lacking supplies. Where the kids are safe and have mentors in leadership roles to guide them to a bright future."

Lee nods. "Sounds like a great idea to me."

As we continue to talk, I don't even know what I'm saying half the time because my heart isn't in this at all, but he responds favorably, slowly pulling me out of my shell by holding my hands and urging me to open up to him.

"So, tell me about your past," I finally say, hoping to not have to think for a little while. "Who was little Lee?"

Lee looks down before replying. "I was the kid who exists in every class, I guess. I was the nerdy kid, the kid who didn't have a lot of friends. Oh, I had friends, I guess, but their names were Master Chief and Mario and The Blue Eyed White Dragon."

I recognize two of those but get his point. "You were a loner?"

"And bullied more than a couple of times," Lee admits. "I just didn't fit in with any particular group. So I made a place to be myself online, talking to a camera instead of people. It was cool because there are so many people online that I found others like me, and they listened to my opinions about something I love. Slowly, I found a little confidence and it helped me grow. I found a place to fit in online, but that's sometimes harder still in person. Except with you . . . somehow, I feel like I fit with you."

When Lee smiles at me, it touches my heart and makes me tear up a little. It's so sweet, but I have to admit that some of the heat between us has been forced on his end and the show itself. I guess I can understand though. I mean, if I'd gone through his childhood, I'd be hot on the trigger too.

It's more of that same heat when Meredith directs us for the good night kiss, and as always, he engulfs me with his fire, holding me tightly to his body. It feels like I'm betraying Hayden, but then I remember that he doesn't appear to see a future for us and this is my chance to see if I can have something positive from this show. So I kiss Lee back, reaching my arms around his neck, and he moans into my mouth. After a moment, he leans back, looking into my eyes. "Let's go to bed."

"Cut! Great job, you two," Meredith calls out, giving me a look like she's proud of me. We close the door behind us, and Lee moves in close to me, his hands on my hips.

"Emily, you drive me fucking crazy with how sexy you are. Lying with you all night, knowing that there's probably cameras in here and I can't go too far, is going to kill me. I'm afraid kissing you all night might be enough to drive me over the edge as it is." He walks me across the room and looks down at me, and I can see the fire in his eyes.

As his hands move to cup my breasts, I remember . . .

cameras. Breathlessly, I whisper in Lee's ear, "We should probably cool it. I'm not that kind of girl."

Lee takes a deep, shuddering breath and I can almost see him willing himself to calm, but he nods once. We climb under the covers, him lying on his back, and he pulls me close so I can rest my head on his chest before he shuts off the lights. He lightly brushes up and down my arm with his fingertips and it feels nice. Maybe not what I've had with Hayden before yesterday, but apparently, that ship has sailed and he was just using me or he freaked out on me. This could work, I guess. And with that thought, I drift off.

CHAPTER 21

EMILY

Confessional

I clear my throat, still torn over what I'm about to say. It's not what I thought I'd be saying just two days ago, when I was fully prepared to say some nice things about Lee and buffer them with praise of Hayden. But that was before, and now I've got Meredith giving me a look that says 'Perform, dancing monkey, time to make the crowd happy.' It's not what I expected when I signed up for this, and by now, I'm more than ready to never watch reality TV again.

I clear my throat again, then talk to the camera. "If I had to sum it up shortly, my date with Lee was perfect. He was interesting, he opened up to me, and he said some things that really touched my heart. I know that Lee comes off like he's always been the man, or whatever you want to call it, but hearing about his past, I understand and was moved. Of course, he was intensely passionate, as he's always been. It feels good that he likes me that much. A line *came to me today from a super-old movie that I caught on cable once,* Revenge Of The Nerds. *'All jocks think about is sports. All we ever think about is sex.' And while that might be a bit crude, if Lee's kissing is any demonstration, there's a lot of truth in that line."*

I make my way to the elevator, but before the door can close, Meredith sticks her hand in, forcing her way inside. Nate, as always, is hovering behind her with his clipboard. Just once, I want to see what he's scribbling on it because I suspect he's just doodling to look like he's actually doing something. There's no way anyone needs to write that much stuff down.

"Meredith, I really—"

As usual, Meredith plows right over me. "All right, production meeting last night was unanimous. You're matching with Lee. I know you weren't certain, but surely, after last night, you can tell that's the way to go. Both for the show and for your heart."

"I . . . I don't know. It's just a lot. Last night was great, but it's hard to let go of everything I've felt with Hayden. I mean, all that you said before makes sense, but I know how I feel."

Meredith sighs, nodding. "I know, honey. But realistically, you don't want Hayden to make a fool out of you. When his confessionals air, and then if you choose him . . . well, that just doesn't look very good for you, does it? Think with your head a bit here. You're a sweet girl, and viewers are gonna see themselves in you. Don't let them down by picking the hottie player when you can pick the self-made man who let himself be vulnerable with you and lights up when you come in the room."

I sigh. Maybe she's right. It does have a sort of ring to it. Not to mention, I'm going to look stupid being played if I choose Hayden, but it just doesn't feel right. It's tearing at my guts and my heart, and the knots in my stomach twist even tighter as I try to sort through my choices. Finally, reluctantly, I agree. "Fine, let's just do this. I just want it to be over with."

"Good. Go get yourself some rest, then get prepped. We're shooting the final elimination at sunset in front of the fountains. You guys can drive off into the sunset that way. It'll be a great shot, trust me."

I nod, my head throbbing at her words. It's not supposed to be like this. I'm not supposed to be riding into the sunset with Lee. A seemingly good man, but a man I don't really have feelings for. Who I really want to be with . . . I guess it doesn't matter.

I head back to my room, where I lie down. I wish I could call Cassie. She'd be able to give me some good advice on all of this. She's as much a reality junkie as I am, and she's got a good head on her shoulders. But we're in total communication silence. I can't even get the damn news, much less a phone call. So instead, I lie back and close my eyes until there's a knock on the bedroom door and McKayla sticks her head in. "Hey, chica, you ready?"

"For what?" I ask miserably. "I just want this shit to be over with."

McKayla comes in, her eyes filled with worry. "Honey, come on, now, it's only a few more hours and then you and your Prince Charming get to climb in that limo and you don't have to hold back on saying you've got feelings for him anymore. Hell, if I had that to look forward to, I'd be jumping up and down and trying to get them to speed the damn time-line up."

I groan, shaking my head. "It's not gonna be that."

"What do you mean . . . oh, shit," McKayla says, sitting down. "You're fucking kidding me."

"What? I had a pretty simple choice, it seemed. On one hand, a guy that I'm falling for but who was totally gaslighting me. And on the other, a guy who's really into me, but I don't have feelings for him. At least I don't look like a fucking idiot choosing the guy who actually likes me."

McKayla purses her lips and looks around the room. "Listen, how do you know he's not really into you? I mean, a few days ago you, both looked so goddamn gaga over each other I was ready to go get a diabetes test."

"I saw some of what he's said in confessional," I admit, and McKayla sighs. "What?"

"You don't think that shit gets edited to angle it a certain way? You know it will. They gotta turn a five-minute confessional into a forty-five-second soundbite. Did you hear all of it?"

"No," I reply, "but he did say he wasn't in love with me. And then he virtually ghosted me on our suite date. And just . . . I made my choice."

"You'd better think more on it!" McKayla says, shutting her mouth when I look at her angrily. "Listen, this whole thing, it touches me, okay? I know, I know, I'm the smart-mouthed bitch who does hair and isn't supposed to give a fuck, but Em, I like you. And I want you to be happy."

"I'd like to be happy too," I admit, sighing. "Now, let's get down to makeup and get ready, or else Brad's gonna bitch and Meredith's gonna bitch even more."

"Wait," McKayla says, grabbing my arm. "Seriously, tell me you're going to think some more on this!"

I look into her eyes, touched by the compassion and the fire burning in them. It's so fierce, it hurts when I nod, swallowing. "I'll do the right thing."

McKayla grins. "Then let's go make you fucking gorgeous."

    I know I look beautiful. Brad and McKayla really outdid themselves in the prep for the final scene, but there's no real pep in my step as I shuffle on set, taking the cards from Nate. "Hey, you okay?" Nate asks, looking at me. "Remember, this is the last chance to make a good impression for the audience. We really need you to deliver."

I nod, and for a moment, I think about what I told McKayla. Do the right thing. But no matter what, there is no right thing. I feel like I'm making the wrong choice either way. Nate looks at me again and turns to say something to Meredith, who I can see is going straight Marie Antoinette on some poor schmuck, but before he can say anything, I reach out and grab his arm. "No. I can do it."

"Okay." Nate says, and I force myself to smile, rolling my shoulders back and hoping that the glitter in my eyes doesn't look too false. I walk onto set, taking my place on the final podium.

"Change of plans," Meredith says, approaching me. "No limo, the LVPD wasn't willing to shut down the street to let us get the shot we wanted. Apparently, Celine Dion's show demands more respect than we do. So after this, we'll have one more scene after nightfall, you two getting into a helicopter and flying off. Very *Fifty Shades*, you know."

"Whatever, I'm good." I see Hayden and Lee come on set, both of them looking stunning in tailored tuxedos, and my heart clenches in my chest. They look their best, with their hair styled perfectly, their jawlines both looking strong enough to crack granite, and their tuxedos making them look like ten million bucks. But in my heart, I know that what I'm about to do . . . it's just not right. But my brain is telling me that if I switch my decision, I'm going to be doing the wrong thing, too. Either way, I lose.

Meredith yells, "Action!" and the cameras start to roll. I see her give me a countdown. I'm sure that right now, they're probably getting voiceover footage for the finale before she waves and points at me. I'm on.

I look between the two men, Lee looking hopeful and sincere and Hayden looking like he's barely controlling some anger below the surface, although I don't know why he's the mad one. Putting on a false smile, I begin to speak. "Talk about a journey. Hayden and Lee, I've had such an experience with each of you and will always treasure the dates we've had. Hayden, whether it was horseback riding, watching you play football, or our private dates in the hot tub and then in the Asian fantasy suite, you've given me memories that will last a lifetime."

"You, too," Hayden replies. "Emily, you're an amazing woman."

I expect him to say more, but he closes his mouth, and I turn to Lee. "Lee, from that first date, you've been the man who turns up the heat. It took me a while to see the real you, but when you opened yourself up to me, I was touched and moved as well."

"Emily, I know it took me a while," Lee says, smiling shyly. "I kept kicking myself after every date we had, saying that I should have opened up more and that I was a fool for being too afraid to do just that. Thank you for the patience you showed me, and I hope that you'll give me the chance to show you more."

"Well, now's the time to find out," I reply. I pause, feeling my nerves bubbling up inside me. I can see the emotions in both of their eyes, their faces lit up by the lights from the fountain. Meredith hollers at me when I take too long, and I quickly swallow my nerves to get on with this. "Hayden, Lee, please step forward. I've thought long and hard about this. So gentlemen, let's see if we're a Match. Please . . . turn over your cards." With a 1-2-3, we turn over, and Lee's face breaks into a huge grin and he swoops forward, picking me up in a hug before I even have a chance to say anything.

"Match made in heaven, Emily!" he says as he spins me around. He's obviously happy, and I try to smile, but my eyes meet Hayden's over Lee's shoulder and lock. His eyes are blazing, and he looks like he's about ready to put his foot right up Lee's ass. He's obviously angry but trying desperately to hide it. Finally, he steps forward and shakes Lee's hand.

"Congratulations, Lee. She's a great woman."

"Thank you. That she is," Lee says. Hayden turns to me, and I see not just anger but something else in his eyes as he gives me a little side hug before turning to walk off-set without even a congratulations or a goodbye.

What the fuck was that? I don't understand what happened to him. We were doing so well and I thought we really had something till he went cold fish on our suite date. Am I really that blind or stupid or both? Apparently so. "Hay—"

Meredith interrupts me, calling out in her loud voice. "Hayden, wait. We need to film the teaser scene before you go inside." *Teaser scene?* What the hell does that mean?

He turns back, looking me dead in the eye but talking to Meredith. I see the anger flaring in his eyes, and a vindictive flash that I know all too well. Hayden's hurt. Why? How? I want to ask him, but he just answers Meredith instead. "Now? I've got the lines memorized, but I didn't think it'd be now. You know what? Fine, let's get it over with." Hayden walks up to a mark just in front of Lee and me, looking in the camera.

"Thank you for watching Season 1 of Matchmaker. It was such a fun roll of the dice, and next season, it'll be my turn. I'll be the Match for thirty new suitors. So ladies, send in your video applications. Are you my match? Guess we'll have to play and see."

I realize what he's said and my stomach plummets as I feel Lee tense beside me. Under his breath, I hear Lee mutter, "What the fuck? That's supposed to be me."

I look up at him, but before I can say anything, Meredith starts clapping loudly. "And that's a wrap, people! Great job, everyone! If you'll head inside to your rooms, we'll be through shortly for final instructions. Lee and Emily . . . get ready for the chopper scene. It'll take you back to Los Angeles. You've got interviews tomorrow."

CHAPTER 22

EMILY

I plop into the chair, McKayla and Brad staring at me open-mouthed. Brad looks like he's about to cry while McKayla just looks pissed off. "What the actual fuck just happened? I thought you said you were going to do the right thing."

Brad puts a hand on McKayla's arm, obviously trying to slow her roll. "I think what McKayla means is . . ." he says, his voice squeaky until he clears his throat, and when he speaks again, there's no hint of the lisp or the silly effeminate makeup artist, but a pissed off guy who's genuinely hurt. "Nope, can't do it. Emily, what the fuck, bitch?"

I look back and forth at them and lose it, tears gushing down my face as I break down. Blubbering, I try to explain that I found out Hayden was playing me, didn't love me, and was gonna make me look like a fool so production had me pick Lee to make the show a *better* ending. McKayla listens for a minute, then sighs. I don't know if she's disgusted, angry, or pitying me. I just know it makes me cry all the harder until she puts her hands on my shoulders, pulling me in and letting me calm down slightly. "Chickadee, I don't know what you saw or what you heard, but I've seen players and I've seen men in love. Hayden would look at you when your back was turned, and his eyes weren't looking like a player. He would talk with the other guys off camera, and every word he said was respectful and full of meaning for you. To top it off, he was begging us for help to have alone time with you off camera. I think you may have been played, just not by Hayden."

I gulp, swallowing back my tears as Brad brings me a cup of coffee, the hot drink helping me calm some. "But what if it was just part of his devious plan to win the show? Get some recognition? It fucking worked, did you hear? The asshole is the lead for next season, so joke's on me." I disintegrate into tears again, Brad being quick to scoop my cup up before I burn myself.

Nate pops his head in the door. "Uh, excuse me, ladies, can I come in?" He steps in, closing the door behind him without waiting for a reply. "Meredith sent me to suggest you pack pink tones for the show in the morning. Quote, 'to make her look flushed and happy' for the interviews. Oh, and sparkly for the chopper shot, wardrobe has a jewel-encrusted pantsuit for her to wear."

Brad turns, a hint of his lisp coming back as he talks to the production assistant. "Thanks. We'll keep that in mind, but kinda busy with a crisis here, Nate. And tell wardrobe to stop dressing Emily like a stripper."

Nate looks at me, obviously uncomfortable. "You okay?"

There's something about his question that pisses me off, which at least clears my tears for a moment. I turn to him, huffing. "No, I'm not okay. And you damn well know it, too. You were there in that meeting and know Hayden played me the whole damn time. I fell for him for real and now my heart is broken."

Nate looks shocked at my outburst and tries to speak, but I'm on a roll now and I need to let the pain out of my soul. "Now I get to go on TV and fake being in love with another man so I don't hurt a bunch of other people. Oh, yeah . . . y'all just keep pulling the puppet strings. I'll go with Lee and do the interviews. I'll do my best to work a smile. But really? I wish I'd never done this show."

McKayla and Brad hug me into them, whispering 'it's okay' and patting my back, shooing Nate out. We get through the prep for the chopper shot, and by keeping the camera behind me most of the time, Meredith's able to get a shot of me and Lee climbing into the chopper together. Inside, Lee's muttered words come back to me, but I've had enough pain for one day. When we get back to LA, we head straight to the hotel. Before my room door even closes, I crawl into bed and pull the covers over my head.

I spent the whole night alternating between pacing and ranting and curling up and crying. By morning, I look like hell, and I feel even worse. McKayla and Brad do their best to perk me up, both with makeup that feels inches thick to cover my red eyes and light jokes to lighten the somberness surrounding me. Whatever drama there might have been last night, and regardless of how exhausted the two of them have to be after driving back to LA, they do their best to cheer me up.

In the green room, Meredith addresses Lee and me. "Okay, guys, the hosts have a set list of approved questions. You just need to answer like lovebirds looking forward to the rest of your lives together without giving away too much. If anything seems too deep, promote the reunion show to find out. Remember, while this is going to be taped, that doesn't mean we want it to be super edited or anything."

"How long until the finale is shown?" Lee asks, and I nod. Maybe we've got different reasons for this, but I have to know how long I have to keep up the happy face charade before I can let it show that I'm broken up inside.

"The delay isn't as bad as some of the shows, only a few weeks," she says. "The reunion show will be filmed the night of the finale, and we'll get you the details on that soon."

A few minutes later, we walk out to hugs from the show hosts, who are acting like it's the middle of the morning instead of one in the afternoon. I guess it's just more of the magic of television. Settling into a couch, I do my best to keep my 'game face' on as the hosts check their question sheets. "Congrats, you two! Sounds like a Match was made for the Matchmaker! Tell me how you're doing."

Lee slips an arm around my shoulders, pulling me close, and I try to look comfortable even as I'm cringing inside. Lee's dressed perhaps more casually than I've seen him except for the physical challenges of the show, in a polo shirt and khakis that make him look . . . kind of suburban. "Well, we had so many great dates and I think I just swept her off her feet. She had to pick me as her Match."

I smile politely, not able to say a word as the hosts give me a lead that I fail to pick up. Finally, the host plows on. "Emily, it seemed like you had several great dates and connections with several suitors. In fact, there'd been lots of chatter, even betting pools, about whom you'd pick. I'll admit that my bet was for Hayden. What happened there?"

I feel Lee tense a little but figure he doesn't want to talk about Hayden when it's supposed to be our promo time. "Yeah, the guys were all really great, some more my type than others. The final two were definitely my frontrunners from the very beginning. It was a hard decision." I take a steadying breath, refusing to cry on fucking TV about Hayden, and I can feel the anticipation in the air as the host waits for more.

The seconds drag out, and Lee takes the opportunity to pull me to him. "She just couldn't deny our chemistry . . ." before he covers my mouth in a kiss, using a finger to tip my chin up to meet his lips. The host makes an oohing sound, and I'm a little relieved at the break from the Hayden subject. After a few more easy questions, we're done.

I am glad to get offstage. I'm so sick of this fakeness that I can't put up with it for one minute longer. I already heard Meredith talking with the producer of the morning show program. They're going to use a 'canned audience' sound for the kiss. This is a huge joke.

Whatever, I know there's a few more interviews to take care of still before Lee and I have to work out the details of how we're going to maintain a relationship with our real lives still going on. It'll be hard. We live on opposite coasts, but I'll be willing to give Lee a fair chance. I mean, I was so head over heels for Hayden that I didn't really give Lee the attention he deserved, and maybe I should.

Back in the green room, though, Lee is visibly frustrated, not quite yelling but definitely a bit loud. "Em, you've got to answer the questions about the suitors better. I can't save you every time. Both of us have a lot riding on these appearances. Get it together and don't fuck this up." I'm shocked and put off, but before I can react, he walks off, shaking his head.

CHAPTER 23

HAYDEN

"*Hey*, Hayden, good to see you again," Meredith says. It's been a week, and I'll admit I've pretty much zombied my way through the past seven days. I go to the gym because I'm supposed to. I talk to Jay because he calls me, but other than that, I just sleep or veg. "How have you been?"

"I've been fine," I reply, tugging at my jeans. Fuck getting dressed up for this.

"Hmm, really? Because I gotta tell you, gorgeous, you look like shit," Meredith says. "I mean, really hot shit, but still shit."

"I think I picked up a bug in Vegas," I lie through my teeth. "You know those buffets aren't the cleanest places, and after filming wrapped, I sorta went on a bender for a day or two while you guys were footing the bill."

"That's just fine. You've got time to get yourself back into shape," Meredith says. "Okay, down to business. Check this out, this will be airing the day after the finale. Edited down, of course. They took a half hour for what's probably going to end up being five minutes on the morning shows."

Meredith picks up a remote on her desk, and the TV mounted on the wall fires up. I get to watch their fucking interview on TV, not wanting to but at the same time forcing myself. I want to see what Emily says about me and the other guys. Hell, I want to see what Lee says.

As the interview continues, I feel my hands clenching in my lap as I listen to Lee. That asshole, figures he'd talk trash. Not just about me, but everyone. He does it in a passive-aggressive way that makes it seem natural, but that's Lee. I took a moment to chat with Dean two days ago, and he explained it best.

"Lee's the straw on the camel's back sort of asshole. None of his comments, by themselves, are worth punching him in the mouth over. But you add them all up, and eventually, you just hate the guy and want to kick his ass. The moment you do, though, he gets to look all innocent and shit because you look like a petty asshole listing a hundred and fifty pieces of pitty-pat shit. And nobody who isn't the target of his words is going to get it. They just laugh it off like it's nothing. But when you're on the receiving end . . . you wanna go Tyson on his ass."

That's Lee to a T. And while he does make a couple of comments about being the best match, he seems to be fully in his "camera personality", not his real self. I saw it too much over the weeks of filming. The guy would save all his backstabbing and his comments for when he knew nobody would be able to call him on his shit.

I wonder if Emily has spotted the difference yet. Nope, I'm stopping that train of thought in its tracks because it doesn't matter. She picked him, not me. And that's all that matters. I wonder if she knew she was gonna pick him even when she was with me. Hell, maybe she fucked him too. I don't think so, but I thought I knew her. Maybe I didn't.

"Hayden?" Meredith asks, and I look over, realizing that the interview's over. "What do you think?"

"I . . ." I start, but before I can half bumble-fuck some answer, my phone rings, and even though I don't want to talk to anyone, I'm grateful. I look down. It's Jay, and I look up at Meredith. "Gimme five minutes to talk with my agent?"

"Jay?" Meredith asks. "Sure. Tell him I said hi, and I'm sending over some contract paperwork to him soon."

I answer in the hallway, leaning back against the wall. "Yo, Jay."

"Hayden, my man! Way to roll a runner-up slot into an even better gig! Listen, I know I'm not supposed to know, but Meredith was nice enough to reach out to me. She showed me some of the early edits on the first few episodes, at least the parts where you're on screen. I didn't think you had it in you, but you were napalm fucking fire on that screen. Women all over the US are gonna be wet for you this fall!"

That's just what I want to hear, Jay, totally makes up for what I've been through. "Yeah, uh . . . thanks, I guess? It played out how it did. I'm not sure I want to do that again though."

There's silence on the other end of the line, and I know Jay's sitting in his office, probably trying not to drop his feet from his desk to the carpet and tip over his coffee. "What are you talking about, Hayden? Of course you're doing it again! It's the best gig you've ever been offered. You're going to be a fucking one-name celebrity right now, and we're capitalizing on that. Hell, you need it. While you've been gone filming,

Frances has been flaming your unprofessional ass all over the industry."

"I know. It's just . . ."

Jay sighs, and this time I can hear his feet come down off his desk. "She fucking got to you, didn't she? Man, I saw the videos. The bitch played you. Don't you dare let that fuck up your career. No way in hell, I'm not letting you do that to yourself."

I can't help but feel a twinge of anger at the words, 'the bitch', but I know he's just trying to show he's got my back, so I shrug it off. I lean back, bumping my head on the wall and rubbing at my eyes. "Just give me some time, okay? We've still got the reunion show to film, and I did actually drag my happy ass down here to talk to Meredith. By the way, she said she's sending you some paperwork or some shit. Maybe after the reunion show, I can move on."

"Uh-uh. No maybe bullshit. After the reunion show, filming starts in three months and you'll have some promo gigs before that. Get your shit straight and get ready. If I need to, I'm gonna pull out the sofa bed in my house and put you into Matchmaker boot camp. You're gonna walk onto that second season set ready to own it."

I sigh. Why is Jay so worked up about this? The modeling contracts? What? "Okay, whatever, man. I'll keep it all in mind."

After Jay gets off the line, I talk to Meredith for a few more minutes. Nothing big, I don't think. I hardly hear anything she says. I'm just going through the motions right now.

"Listen, here's some of the girls we rejected for the first season. We already reached out to them, asked if they would be interested in being in Season Two. Take a look through the videos. Get back to us if there's any, in particular, you might want to see on the show."

Leaving the studio, I look at the flash drive, tempted to throw it into the street. I don't know if I can do this . . . any of this. I need to talk to someone about all of this, but I signed a fucking NDA. Fuck it, I know someone who'll keep quiet and listen to me. I ride back to my apartment and load up the saddlebags of my Harley before hitting the road.

I drive all night, pulling into my childhood home just as the morning sun is rising over the horizon. The lights are already on, and as I shut off the loud bike, the door opens, my mom smiling warmly at me. She's dressed for work, looking a little surprised as she sticks her head out of the ranch-style house I grew up in. The paint's a little faded, but Mom looks just like she did when I last saw her six months ago.

"Hayden? Baby, you surprised the shit out of me! Get in this house before the neighbors start yelling about the racket at this time of morning."

Bending down to give her a big hug, I finally feel myself relax. Five minutes later, I'm sitting down at the table, coffee in front of me, my mom and dad both giving me inquisitive looks as I poke at the plate of bacon and eggs with toast that Mom put together for me. Dad sets his cup down before giving me a tentative smile. "Good to see you, Son. I gotta ask you, though, what brings you here with no call at six in the morning?"

I thought, as I was riding, that talking about the show would be easy. But sitting here, at the same wood table where I ate countless meals, the same wood table where I learned I'd have to have surgery, and the same wood table where I gave up on baseball forever, I find it hard to talk about. The words come slowly, haltingly at first. Mom and Dad are patient though, listening as I tell them about Frances, about the cattle call for *Matchmaker*, and about the show itself.

"And you really have feelings for this young lady?" Dad asks.

"Something just clicked with us, and it was like no matter what, I wanted to see her, talk to her. I mean, I risked getting kicked off the show over it with all the sneaking around we did. I thought it was mutual, I really did. But I found out I was wrong."

"What do you mean?" Mom asks worriedly, and I realize she and Dad are going to be late for work. She glances at the clock and gets up, grabbing the phone and going into the living room. She comes back five minutes later, hanging the phone up. "I called in. We're taking a half day off. Family emergency."

Her simple, unadorned sign of love touches me and I have to clear my throat before I continue. "The producer showed me the videos," I explain. "Emily and Lee, their confessionals, their . . . dates. It was like a knife in the gut. And so I took the deal Meredith offered. They want me to be the Match for next season."

Mom nods like she understands while Dad looks a little perplexed. Then again, his idea of reality television has usually involved touchdowns and strikes. Mom reads him perfectly and explains it quickly to him while I finish my coffee, Dad sitting silently through it all before he speaks.

"I saw the ads. The premiere episode is supposed to be on tomorrow. I watched what I could just because I knew you were in it, Son. One of the girls at the office told me."

"Thanks, Dad, sorry to ruin the ending," I reply. "Guess you can spend that time watching *Baseball Tonight*."

"Perhaps, but there was something I saw," Dad says. "Hayden, they showed a lot of the kissing. I guess they wanted to up the heat in the preview or something. Lee, I'm guessing he's the slick looking one?" When I nod, Dad shakes his head. "Well, one thing I noticed, she never kisses him. He always kisses her for the most part. In the five-minute preview they stuck on the network last week, it seemed like he was the one pushing the issue every time. Seems a little convenient to me."

"Okay, so what are you getting at here, Dad?"

He smiles softly, the same sort of smile he'd get when he was my Little League coach and his hard-headed son was missing something in the game that he knew would be obvious once he explained it right. "No, just seems to me that you thought y'all had something real, and maybe you did, maybe you didn't. But Lee seems like he's swooping in all Prince Charming-like, and that's hard to resist, especially when you don't see you're getting set up. Did Emily seem particularly cunning? Skeptical?"

I shake my head, still not quite getting it. "No, she's sweet, seemed a little uncomfortable about the whole thing initially. But she seemed to play the game in the end."

Dad leans back in his chair, rubbing at his receding hairline which I swear I've added at least an inch to over the years. "Okay, let me put it more plain. Who's the most likely one to get played by a game show . . . you, Lee, or Emily?"

I realize what he's saying, understanding dawning. Emily. She'd be the one to get played. She's just too sweet and wouldn't suspect that of someone. But how? What's Lee's payoff? Dad raises his coffee mug to me, saluting. "Just a little something to mull over in that big head of yours. If you have feelings for her, tell her. Maybe she did play you, but you'll never know unless you try. Find out if you misread things or if you both got played."

CHAPTER 24

EMILY

*A*fter going back home, I hate being in Los Angeles. It's a week before the reunion show films, and starting tomorrow, I'm supposed to have a bunch of interviews coming up. The show's been on for over a month now, and all I want to do is disappear into my bed and sleep. I want to pretend the whole thing never happened. Everyone has been supportive, and my friend Cassie was as helpful as she could have been, but I just couldn't explain to anyone how weird the whole situation was.

Part of it is how cold and distant Lee's been. After that incident with the interview, other than for public appearances, we barely talk to each other. He hasn't been to see me and we haven't even Skyped. The few times I have talked to him, he always has this . . . I don't know what to call it, just a slightly annoyed tone to his voice, like I'm keeping him from something he would rather be doing instead. When I invited him out to spend some time with me, he turned me down, saying that he had some kind of business convention to attend.

McKayla and Brad have both called me, trying to talk me

through the whole thing. They still don't understand what happened with Hayden, and to be honest, I don't either, so I can't answer them. I told McKayla about Lee almost yelling at me to get it together after the interview and she offered to cut his balls off and feed them to him. "A for-reals ball gag, get it?"

I huffed but couldn't really laugh and told her I'd keep the offer in mind. I've been binge-watching the show, even though it makes me cry every time I see Hayden on screen. The rest of the guys are interesting, surprising me several times in their confessionals. Some of them were much trickier than I thought, obviously hoping for screen time and talking up ways to seduce me. I'm glad they didn't get much of a chance. I do feel bad for Dean though. While I never had a real connection with him, I do think he's just about the sweetest guy in the whole bunch. I really wish I could have had more one-on-one time with him. I still don't think we would have had a love connection, but he's an interesting guy and I think we could be friends.

For most of the season, Hayden and Lee's confessionals have been pretty similar, both talking about how much they like me, our connection, and how much fun we have. It's hard to watch myself date and kiss and interact with them, making me feel stupid again for being blind to their games. I'm in full pity-party mode when I hear a tap at my door. I sit up. I'm not supposed to be meeting with anyone until tomorrow, and I know the studio didn't put my name on the hotel reservation. Who could it be?

Peeking through the hole, I see McKayla and Brad, along with a third person in a hoodie pulled up high enough I can't see their face. I crack the door open. "Guys, what are you doing here? How did you even get here? I can't right now, I just can't."

Ignoring the whine in my voice, McKayla pushes the door open, barging in. "Sit down and listen up, babe. You'll want to hear this shit."

Brad follows her in, and as the door shuts, the third person pulls down their hoodie, and I see it's Nate. I tilt my head, surprised for a moment. I've never seen him in anything as 'low-brow' as a hoodie. He looks almost normal right now. "Nate? What are you doing here?"

Before he can say anything, Brad interrupts. "Alcohol. Where's your good stuff because you're gonna need it for this."

I point to the mini-fridge, waving my hand. "The minibar's got some stuff. I haven't really checked exactly what."

Brad goes over, squatting down in his pink stretch jeans and humming to himself as he roots around before coming out with three bottles. "Tequila it is. Sit."

Brad cracks open the seal and pours the whole contents into one of the tumblers before putting in two ice cubes and setting a shot in front of me, crossing his arms over his skinny chest. "Drink the whole thing. Then Nate-boy here talks."

At this point, I'm scared not to because McKayla looks especially pissed as hell and I don't know why. I drink it all, the Jose Cuervo burning on the way down to bloom like fire in my stomach. Blinking and hoping I won't be shitfaced in ten minutes, I look at the trio. "All right, consider me prepped. Now what's this all about?"

McKayla and Brad sit on either side of me on the bed,

looking at Nate, and he shifts in the chair across from us. Finally, after a glare from McKayla that would turn most men to stone, he starts talking. "Okay, so first of all, I was never here. I'm not losing my job for this. Meredith would have my heart for dinner if she knew I was even talking to you. But I see things, hear things. Nobody even notices me because I'm just background, like scenery."

I nod like I know what he's talking about. I mean, most of the filming, everyone just sort of dismissed him as Meredith's lapdog, her bitch boy who ran around delivering messages more than anything else. "Go on."

"I was sitting in when Meredith got a call from Lee's social media manager."

"Uh, what? Lee's got a social media manager?" I ask, raising an eyebrow. "I didn't know that. Actually, I don't even know what that is."

"He didn't get all those Instagram fans and YouTube subscribers on his own," Nate replies, making me feel like an idiot. "Basically, he told Meredith that he was preparing a total social media onslaught against the show if Lee didn't come out looking like a million bucks. He didn't go into specifics, but after the scandal *Bachelorette* had down in Mexico, Meredith didn't want to take any chances. She said she'd make sure Lee either won or got to the finals so that he could be the next season's match."

"That bitch!" I exclaim, but McKayla holds up a hand.

"Hold your horses. There's more," she says, patting my leg. "Go on, Nate."

"Meredith started manipulating things. She saw how Hayden was doing so great in the test audiences so she wanted him to be the next Match. It'd give the next season the best chance at success. So she had the tech guys start playing with the equipment, Lee and Hayden getting the solo dates, stuff like that. But she doesn't take well to being threatened, and she didn't want to deal with Lee's douchebaggery again, so she did what she could to ensure he won, upholding her deal with the manager but minimizing Lee's overall future with the show. His team was the one that had that ringer kid in football. She edited the confessionals and the test audience . . . stuff to make him look like a dreamboat. At the meetings, she told both Lee and Hayden they'd be the Match if they weren't picked."

"So it was rigged?" I ask, aghast, and Nate shrugs. "You asshole."

"It was clean-ish until that meeting, pretty standard scripting for a reality show. But in that meeting, Lee was like a kid in a candy store, going on and on about his fans and how they'd be his most loyal viewers. Hayden had to be threatened with his contract, though, and Meredith made a decision. She knew you two were hitting it off for real, and she couldn't deal with Lee's bullshit again. It wasn't worth the risk. Viewers could find out what he's really like and flip on him in an instant. So she had me put together some edited clips of your dates with Lee, making it look like you two were all over each other and you were just playing Hayden. On the other side, she had me edit Hayden's next confessional to try and make him look bad."

Nate stops, looking at all of us to get our reactions. "Go on," Brad says in a threatening voice. "Or a certain video of you might just surface."

Nate gulps, then continues. "Even then, it took a few confessions to get the right sound bites out of Hayden," Nate says.

"And we tweaked the fantasy dates. Right before, Meredith reminded Hayden that he needed to cool it a bit with you. Nobody's interested in a rebound guy who just lost the girl he wanted when she picks someone else. That's why Hayden was off on your date. He thought you were all cozy with Lee and just playing him for the cameras."

"And I thought he was cooling on me," I whisper, tears coming to my eyes. "I thought he got freaked out by something I said."

"Yeah, well, you both got played . . . by Meredith and Lee."

"Wait, I get how Meredith is the bad guy here and Lee might've forced Meredith's hand a bit, but how did he play me too?"

Nate looks guiltier than ever, shaking his head. "Meredith was meeting with him, sharing tips from your confessionals so he knew where he was doing well and where to improve so he could be what you want. I thought, watching your dates, that you'd have a fling and a breakup, get a bit of publicity, and have a little fun. It's not like anyone comes on these shows to actually fall in love for real. But he was just hoping to get as much out of your picking him as he can. And when Meredith told him to shut you up anytime you asked questions, he did. Didn't it seem like he just kissed you out of nowhere sometimes?"

I think about it, nodding. "Well, yeah, but I thought he was just the aggressive type. He kept telling me how much he wanted me, how I drove him crazy . . ." I reply before realizing how royally I've fucked things up and how I've lost Hayden. Groaning deeply, I feel like I'm about to throw up when Brad and McKayla put their arms around me. "Oh,

Jesus. Guys, what am I going to do? I mean, I could've really had something with Hayden."

Almost simultaneously, Nate, McKayla, and Brad state together, "Reunion show."

McKayla chuckles a little at the harmony before grinning widely "Where the players get played. Muahaha."

Brad looks over, grinning. "That's a pretty legit villain laugh you've got there. Too bad we're the good guys."

McKayla shrugs. "Good guys, bad guys . . . fuck all that. They fucked with my chica. I'm vengeance come to life, like a horror movie. You can't escape."

For the first time in days, I smile. A real one, and I laugh at their antics and mentally get myself ready to set shit straight on national TV. Suddenly, a thought comes to me. "Wait . . . what's this about a video of you, Nate?"

Nate looks nervous again but Brad waves it off. "Nothing you need to worry about, honey. Nate knows he did the right thing, so the Karma Fairy is going to reward him."

I guess some things I just don't need to know.

CHAPTER 25

EMILY

Sitting backstage in my private dressing room, my hands are trembling. I've done all the interviews, keeping up the front so that no one, especially the producers of the show, can get a preview of what's going to happen. Thankfully, Lee's been doing his own thing, and I haven't had to interact with him at all. Other than a few swapped texts, I haven't heard from him since coming back into town. If anything, it only reinforces the feelings I have for what I'm going to do.

Still, it's all I can do to wait to see Hayden. I've considered sneaking into his dressing room a million times, but I have to wait to do this right. I'm gonna throw this whole shit show out in the open on live TV. They're filming it right after the finale airs. I may be sweet and even naïve, but I'm not a doormat, even if I've felt like one during this whole ordeal. I've got some devious friends who know how to make some drama, and I'm on board to do what I need to so I can have a chance to really choose the right man.

Lee pops into my room, looking happier than ever. Guess

he's gotten some more Instagram followers. "Hey, babe, wanted to make sure you were ready for this. You need help with your lines or anything?" He reaches for my hand, acting like he actually cares, and I pull back. He looks at me, tilting his head. "What's up?"

"You barely talk to me all week and ignored me the whole time I was home. Now you want to call me babe and ask about my lines? Just save it."

Lee looks angry, like someone just took his favorite toy away from him, and I wonder for a moment if that's all I've ever been, a toy. "Fine. Just wanted to help. Look, just follow my lead and we'll be fine. Don't fuck this up again."

He leaves, and I take a moment to wonder at how quickly he's gone from sweet and romantic, saying all the right things to get me to fall for his bullshit, to . . . this. He's abrupt and cold, and I realize that this is the real him. I can't believe I didn't see it before because now, it's so obvious. I really wish I could have seen the other confessionals from the other guys, or at least been able to interact with everyone without Meredith's tinkering. I'm sure I would have still fallen for Hayden, but I could have given some other, more deserving guy the chance to get to know me and maybe have a chance to be what Hayden is now, the Season Two Match.

No time to worry about that now. I walk out to set, Brad giving me a discreet thumbs-up while McKayla flips me off with a wink. I know she's not telling me to fuck off, but instead is encouraging me to fuck some shit up, and I smile back. I see Nate next to Meredith but ignore him as he asked me to. I don't want to give it away that he's told me anything. I still don't know what the armlock Brad and McKayla have on him is, but I don't care. He did the right thing in the end.

Sitting down on two rows of couches, the show starts with the audience clapping loudly. The first half of the finale has just aired, where we've come to Vegas and I've had my fantasy dates. Now, of course, everyone gets to watch as the final confessionals and the final Match are made.

I see Hayden, and he keeps glancing at me like he wants to say something. There's a fire in his eyes that I didn't see in Vegas, and I recognize the same look in mine from the mirror this morning. I don't know what his plans are, but I don't care if he's supposed to be the next season's Match or not. If I have to, I'm going to tackle him right here on stage and cover him in kisses if that's what it takes.

All of the top ten guys are here, with the host asking them questions while the show is going through the slow parts that are meant to draw out the tension and draw out the advertisers' money. It's weird, listening to the host ask questions to all the suitors. The guys all talk about me like I'm not sitting right on the other side of the semi-circular stage, an empty spot next to me for the 'big reveal'.

Most of them are complimentary, but there are a few snide remarks, mostly from frat-boy wannabes Mark and Luke, who are still whining about how they didn't realize the mics would pick up their comments. I shake my head, glad I cut them.

I smile a little as I look over at Hayden, remembering . . . well, not *quite* everything.

Finally, the final scene shows, the audience clapping their asses off as Lee comes over and sits down beside me. The host turns all of her questions to the final two suitors. I glance off stage, where I see McKayla draw her thumb across her throat. *Go for the kill.*

I clear my throat to get ready to lay it all out there, but before I can, Lee jumps up. He turns to the camera, holding out his hand. "Wait, guys. First, I have something to say." He drops to one knee, holding up a ring box, and the audience goes wild. "Emily, I never thought I'd find my Match on a game show, but I did. I love you. Marry me. We can even make it air as a special episode for the audience." He turns to the audience to hype them up, like he's some sort of pro wrestler working the crowd. "Would you like that?" They cheer again. Lee turns back, trying to slide the ring onto my finger.

"Wait, wait—" I try to protest, but Lee's grabbed my wrist in a steely grip, and I can barely move. Finally, I curl my finger, anything to keep him from shoving that damn thing on my hand.

Lee glares daggers at me, muttering under his breath, "Follow my lead. It's perfect."

I look back and him and then at Hayden, who looks like he's about to jump out of his chair, held back maybe only by the fact that this could be on live TV. "Wait, I have something to say—"

Lee interrupts, pulling me close to kiss me, forcing his lips on me before pulling back and grinning at the host and the audience. "Look, everyone, she's so taken with the whole thing."

Across the stage from me, I hear Cody, who's been sort of quiet most of the show, speak up. "Seems like the woman has something to say, Lee, so why don't you be quiet and let her talk?"

I glance over, and while he's smiling at Lee, it's decidedly menacing. Lee notices as well and lets me go, rising from his kneeling pose. I give Cody a nod of thanks and get out of my seat to address the audience. Off camera, Meredith's about ready to have a fit, but she can't interrupt, she knows that. "You know, I started this show just like you, a home viewer who thought an adventure on a reality TV show would be the experience of a lifetime. I mean, I'm not what the producers made me sound like. I'm no budding leader in education or whatever it was. I'm just a nanny who likes taking care of three precious little kids and loved getting my daily dose of drama. So *Matchmaker* sounded like a lot of fun. And it was. Until I was given a peek behind the green curtain and saw just how ugly and manipulative it can be."

The audience is quiet, looking at each other uncertainly. The host keeps glancing off set and holding her finger up to her ear, probably being relayed information from Meredith or someone from the network who's off camera. I don't care. This isn't for the home audience. This is for me and for the truth. "I went on dates with these guys, with producers and camera crew and more folks all around. It's never private. Even those supposedly private, intimate moments have hidden cameras. And Meredith, the producer, is telling us what to say, how to react. And I get that. It's her job to make sure she gets the scenes she needs. But is it her job to manipulate us behind the scenes? Telling us a narrative that she's created, showing us confessionals that never aired because she psyched us out, telling us what others said and did, making us believe something that wasn't true? That's what this show is."

There's a few boos from the audience, and even a couple of the guys look outraged. Dean and Cody, in particular, look like they're about to rip someone's head off. I turn to Lee, who's turning blotchy, his cheeks bright red but his forehead almost bloodless while his eyes look shadowed. "You know what, Lee? I found out the truth about you. How you threatened the show with your social media fans, that you'd make a scandal to derail the show even before it got started."

"I . . . that's a damned lie—" Lee starts, his face going surly. "Babe—"

"Let me finish!" I yell, getting angry now. "I'm not going to marry you, not on some special episode, not ever. You tried to hurt people. You lied, most of all, to me! You tried to ruin my chance to find love, to find someone, and why? To get a few more social media fans?"

Lee looks like he's about to explode, and he stands up, jabbing a finger in my direction. "You stupid bitch. You're ruining everything I worked for. It's always about you, you, you. You know what? I was supposed to be the Match next season, that's what. I was gonna break up with you, total sob story, of course, and be the heartbroken heartthrob looking for a second chance. And then Mr. Top Fucking Model went and fucked that up, too!"

Lee lunges at Hayden, but Dean cuts him off him with a nifty little move that's so quick I can't even understand what he's doing. All I know is that Dean steps between Lee and me, they spin, and suddenly, Lee's guided rather forcefully into his seat again, where Cody's ready to clap his huge ham hock-like hands on his shoulders. Dean looks at me shyly, giving me a half-smile. "Never had the chance to tell you . . . third-degree black belt in Aikido."

I give Dean a hug and turn back to Hayden, who's stood up at the general commotion. Meredith is wildly gesturing for a commercial break, but the host is loving this and waves me on. I turn to Hayden, crossing the space and standing in front of him, reaching out and taking his hands.

"And you. I fell for you, hook, line, and sinker. Not some

showbiz version, but for the real you. And as much as I was tricked by Lee's scheming and Meredith's manipulations, you were too, and I hope you realize that. Because I love you, Hayden. Show be damned—hell, everything be damned. I love you."

I stand there, holding my breath, waiting for him to respond. It feels like forever. I don't hear anything for a long time until there's a small cough and the host breaks the silence. "Hayden?"

He holds my hands tighter, but I don't feel the controlling power that Lee was trying to overwhelm me with, but the same strength that Hayden's always had. He doesn't force himself on me as much as reassure me. "I knew you were dating us all. That was the point," he says, not looking anywhere but in my eyes. "But by the pond that night, something changed and I started falling for you. For real. I guess just seeing the dates set me back. I wasn't ready for it. And when you said I was just some bad boy fantasy you were playing out, I thought you were just using me."

I interrupt, blinking. "Bad boy fantasy? Wait, the confessional where I had to say something bad about you?" He looks surprised, nodding, and I look up into the studio lights, starting to laugh before I look him in the eyes again. "Yeah, Meredith had me film a confessional saying good and bad things about each contestant so they could slip them in as needed throughout the season. The worst thing I could come up with for you was that you're my bad boy fantasy come to life and that you could easily break my heart, because I'd already given it to you."

Someone in the audience 'whooooos' and there's a general chuckle around the room as Hayden grins. He steps closer, and the audience lets out another ooooh worthy of a group of middle-schoolers. "That's what you said before they edited it?"

I wrap my arms around his neck, nodding, smiling, and blinking back tears in my eyes all at the same time. "Yes, and you broke my heart, just like I predicted."

Hayden sweeps that same damn curl behind my ear again and touches his forehead to mine, lowering his voice to the point that I wonder if the cameras can pick up the sound at all. I really don't give a shit though. "I'm sorry. I thought you were breaking mine. I love you too."

For an instant, we just look into each other's eyes and then we kiss. From far away, I hear Cody laugh in his signature drawl. "Finally. Took y'all damn near long enough. That's the problem with you city people. Talk, talk, talk. Like Elvis said, *little less conversation, little more action!*"

As we pull apart, the interviewer, ever astute, asks, "Uhm, you said by the pond? What date was that, because we never saw a pond date?" Our eyes widen, realizing we just told on ourselves, and we laugh.

"Yeah . . . uh, that wasn't part of the show."

CHAPTER 26

HAYDEN

*M*eredith is fuming, storming onto set and screeching at everyone as soon as the lights on the cameras go dark. "Go to fucking commercial, why is that so hard? You literally just ruined an entire season." She spots Emily and me, stomping over. "You two, I will have your heads on a plate. You signed contracts to follow direction, not sneak around, ruining my show."

"So what?" I comment as she rants and raves. "Sue me. I've got nine hundred dollars in my checking account. You can have every cent."

We just smile, turning to each other for another kiss. Meredith opens her mouth, but before she can say anything, Nate taps her on the shoulder to get her attention. Meredith turns like a snake, nearly snapping at him. "What?"

Nate holds up his phone, pointing at something on the screen. "Look . . . social media is blowing up about the surprise twist ending. They're loving it. Nobody seems shocked about the production stuff, just excited about the love. Hayden was always the favorite, so people are glad he got the girl. In fact, #EmiHay is the top trending hashtag right now."

"EmiHay?" Dean asks, shaking his head. "Damn, that's terrible."

Meredith fumes, glaring at his phone for a moment until her phone rings. She answers, her face pinching as she hears the voice on the other end of the line. "Yes, sir. Quite the twist. It seems to be going over even better than expected." There's a deep pause, and the caller adds their two cents before Meredith speaks again. "Yes, it does seem we'll have to find another Match for season two, but with this type of publicity, we'll have of the best of the best. Next season is sure to be a hit." She glares at us once more and turns, striding off in a huff. I see Nate glance back, giving Emily a smile.

I pull Emily close, chuckling. "Someone else I should worry about?"

Emily laughs, pulling me tighter. "Nope, just a friend of a friend wishing us well, I think."

I lift her in my arms, ignoring everything else in the studio as I look into her beautiful eyes. "Say it again."

Emily smiles back at me, biting her lip playfully. "What? That I love you? That what you want to hear?"

I growl, swinging her around and shaking her like a puppy. "Woman . . ."

"Hayden, I love you," Emily says, stroking my cheek as I set her down. "I'm sorry that I let myself be talked into saying anything else. Can you forgive me?"

I take her hand, kissing her fingers before lifting her chin to look into my eyes. "We forgive each other, because I fucking love you too."

I cover Emily's mouth in a kiss that quickly grows deeper, and the first sound I hear is a single sharp clap. It takes me a moment to realize it's applause, and our worlds are turned upside down as another set of hands joins, then another, until we're surrounded by a wall of cheers and applause.

We're mid-kiss when I hear someone clearing their throat right next to us. I lift my middle finger, refusing to stop kissing Emily. There's a pleased laugh, and I hear McKayla's voice in our ears. "Fuck off yourself too, but just thought you'd want to know that there's a storage room off the hallway in the back of the soundstage. It even locks . . . if you're interested."

I pull back at her comment, looking at McKayla and giving her a nod of thanks. "Tell everyone that we're gonna need a few."

I grab Emily by the hand, the two of us almost scampering off in the direction McKayla indicated and earning another ooh from the audience. I don't pay them any attention, just needing to be alone with Emily. Slamming the door behind us, I kiss her again, moaning into her mouth.

I know I should be taking my time, but I can't. The emotional roller coaster we've been on is too much. "Fuck, Emily, I need to be inside you. I can't wait," I groan as I hurriedly undo my belt, my cock aching inside my pants. I lift her up and deposit her on a table—who the fuck knows what it's here for, but it's just the right height.

Instead of protesting, Emily lifts her hips, pulling up her skirt and pushing her panties to the side as she does. "I need you, Hayden. Take me, give me what I've been missing."

The heat and hunger in her eyes and voice tell me everything I need to know, and with a fast shove of my pants, I enter her in one thrust. It's hard, fast, pounding her as I growl into her ear, "God, you feel good. I've missed you . . . missed this tight pussy. It's mine, Emily. You're mine."

She gasps and meets my thrusts and my dirty words, digging her fingernails into my arms as she hisses in pleasure. "Yes, that's it. All yours. And you're mine, too."

I reach down, rubbing her clit, demanding that she come on my cock and let me feel her pussy flutter around me. She's jolted by the intense sensation, staring into my eyes as I pound her and stroke her clit. In what feels like an instant, her entire body convulses, her pussy squeezing me tight. It's so fucking sexy, and suddenly, I'm on the edge, my cock about to explode. "Fuck, Emily . . ."

She pulls back, pushing me away to slide off the table and drop to her knees. "No condom . . . so come in my mouth, Hayden. Fuck my mouth and give it to me." Grabbing my hips, she engulfs me with her warm mouth, sucking me in deep, letting me down her throat as I groan. Just a few bobs and I'm done, shouting my release as I hold her head steady with my cock deep in her throat as she swallows every drop.

When I let go, I pull her to her feet, kissing her again tenderly, not even caring because I'm so worked up.

We're adjusting our clothes when there's a knock on the door. "Go away!"

"It's Brad," a familiar voice says from the other side of the door. "Open up, please?"

I glance back at Emily, who gives me a nod as she smooths out her skirt. I open the door to see a smirking Brad, looking me up and down. "What do you need, Brad? We were about to come back out there."

"Yeah . . . everyone knows," Brad says, reaching forward and plucking the tiny wireless mic off my shirt.

I can't help it. I don't know what the hell to say so I just laugh. "Uhh, so everyone heard?"

"The producers cut the feed, but we could hear it at the sound board. You guys fuck like jackrabbits, you know. Now get out of here, out the back before someone wants you to do a special-edition episode or something."

Emily grabs my hand, entwining our fingers and grinning. "Thanks, Karma Fairy."

CHAPTER 27

EMILY

I wake up in the hotel bed, feeling Hayden's warmth behind me. It's been awhile since we've been out to Los Angeles again, but I've gotta admit, I love the feeling of having a five-star bed and Egyptian cotton sheets. I wiggle my ass back against him, feeling him stiffen already. Hayden stirs, putting a strong arm around me and pulling me closer, nuzzling at my neck. "Woman, I was trying to sleep a little more. You waking me up for a reason?"

I take his hand and bring him up to cup my breast, sighing happily when his fingers start stroking my nipple to full stiffness. "Definitely waking you up for a reason. We've got to get ready. But not for a bit longer."

Turning over, I look him in his soulful eyes that are full of lust and bite my lip. Reaching down, my hand still trembles as I find his cock and wrap my hand around him as he grows rock hard and throbbing. Hayden grins wolfishly, cupping my ass and squeezing. "Sleep is so overrated."

Pulling me on top of him, he kisses my neck, nibbling and

licking my skin as his fingers stroke my back before working his way down to wrap his lips around my nipple, tugging at it with his teeth and making my body tremble with need. I grab the headboard, glad we're in a hotel room because after last night, I want more than my poor bed back home could handle. Hayden's tongue and lips tease my nipple until I'm wet and aching between my legs before switching to the other side, stars shooting across my vision as I hold myself still for him.

"Hayden," I moan, reaching down and running my fingers through his hair. "Oh, my love."

Hayden pulls back, looking up at me with a naughty twinkle in his eyes. "My love. That reminds me, I had an idea."

"What's that?" I ask, loving the feeling of his hands on my back as they stroke down to cup my ass. "Let me guess, you want me to tie you up and then find my favorite sex toy?"

Hayden stops, then laughs. "McKayla's been a bad influence on you. No, actually, I was just thinking that I wanted to taste you."

"Hmm, well my favorite number is sixty-nine," I purr, climbing off Hayden just long enough to let him slide down the bed before I climb over his face, lowering my pussy slowly toward him as I reach out and take his cock in my hand. "Now promise me—"

Words are wiped from my mind as the tip of Hayden's tongue starts stroking my pussy lips, making me gasp and pleasure shoot up my spine. I lean forward, pulling his cock to my hungry mouth and engulfing as much as I can, desperate to give him the same feelings he's giving me. Unfortunately, Hayden's so much taller that I can't swallow him fully, but still I bathe the head of his cock with my tongue, sucking and licking it until Hayden arcs his hips, driving more of it into my hungry mouth.

I nearly scream in ecstasy when Hayden finds my clit and nibbles on it, overwhelmed at how good it feels. I moan around his cock until I can't take any more and sit up, grinding my pussy down onto his hungry lips and begging for him to make me come. Hayden reaches around and grabs my ass, not letting me have even an inch of breathing room as he buries his tongue deep inside me, tongue fucking me as his lower lip strokes against my clit over and over. I reach down, planting my hands on his rock hard stomach as the first tremors roll through me. I let myself go, riding and bucking on his tongue until I come, throwing my head back and crying out his name, the most perfect word I can think of.

"Your turn," I tell him when I can speak again, getting off his glistening face, but Hayden doesn't move, instead reaching down and positioning his cock so that it points straight up. "Oh, really?"

"Ride me, cowgirl," Hayden teases. "You know I love it when you do."

Grinning, I turn and climb on top of Hayden, letting my pussy lips tease the head of his cock for a moment as we look into each other's eyes before I sink down slowly, moaning as I feel him stretch me open.

Hayden lets out a deep moan as I envelop him, rolling my hips as I ride him. He reaches up, and we entwine our fingers as I look into his eyes, bouncing up and down before rolling my pussy back and forth, squeezing and moaning as his cock thrusts deep inside me. "You're so fucking perfect, Emily."

"You keep saying that," I reply, smiling as I squeeze his cock again before doing a new little move that Cassie told me about, twerking my hips up and down in bed and making Hayden whimper. It feels so good for us both. "Keep doing it."

I ride him faster and faster, letting go of his hands to put my hand over his heart as he does the same to me, both of us panting. Sweat trickles down my skin, and Hayden starts thrusting up to meet me, our hips slapping together in the early morning light until I feel him swell. "Babe . . ."

"Do it!" I gasp, squeezing him. We've just started it, and I love the feeling as Hayden shudders before his eyes roll up and he comes deep inside me. The sensation pushes me over and I come again, biting my lip hard as I tremble and squeeze him, not wanting a single drop of his precious seed to escape me. Sure, I might be on the pill still, but it doesn't really matter. We'll cross that bridge when we come to it.

I collapse onto Hayden's chest, letting him wrap his arms around me and hold me close as our hearts slow down. After a few minutes, I kiss his chest, looking up at him. "Are you sure we're doing the right thing? I'm scared they're gonna trick us somehow."

Hayden strokes my back, kissing the top of my head before replying, "I know, babe, and maybe someone will try to trick us. I mean, it's been four months and the press is still hounding us. The best way to get everyone off our backs is to do one special interview, answer their questions, and then tell them to leave us alone. We can do this . . . together. No tricks, just answer and get it over with, and then we can get on with our lives."

He's right, and I know it. I'm just nervous and don't trust Meredith or anyone from the media. The way the producers and some of the media tried to drag us through the mud was really shitty in the aftermath of the reunion show, and I've been called a wishy-washy slut on the cover of more tabloids than I can count. For a while, I had to stop shopping at one of my favorite local stores because of the number of magazines with my name and face plastered on the front of them.

But the fans have been great, mostly telling me that I should've picked Hayden all along and blasting the production for playing favorites for ratings. Still, the Season Two premiere numbers don't lie, and all of those same fans telling me they hate how I got played are totally watching.

Yeah, Season Two . . . a full season pickup this time, although not with Hayden. And not with Lee either, which apparently pissed him off enough to post a rant on his YouTube channel that went viral. He went full nutso as he tried to play the jilted lover, but most folks now see him as the conniving player who almost manipulated his way to a win. The last time I cared to check, he'd lost half of his Instagram followers, and most of those who left seem to enjoy flaming the hell out of anything he posts.

The Season Two Match is actually Cody, and I wish him well. Maybe he'll find someone. I just hope he's careful. That big body with all those muscles and Southern drawl is one thing, but I got the feeling, watching the premiere episode, that there are more than a few gold diggers in the bunch.

With a sigh and crossed fingers, we get up and get ready, arriving at the studio just a few minutes before call time. McKayla and Brad are there to do my hair and makeup. I'd planned to just use the studio team, but Brad had acted completely offended that I would dare let someone else touch my face, telling me that they'd be here with bells on . . . quite possibly, literally, knowing him.

The first thing McKayla does when she sees me is give me a big hug, squeezing me so tightly I think my damn ribs are going to crack. "Damn, girl, we do still talk on the phone, you know. I ain't a stranger!"

"Yeah, well, I haven't seen you in months and you're the most normal friend I have. Brad doesn't count."

I laugh, giving Brad a hug too. "You behaving yourself?"

Brad laughs, giving me a kiss on each cheek. "Now you know better than that."

"I guess I should know that," I tease back, sitting down.

"All right, my little chickadee . . . time to make you fabulous!" McKayla says with a grin, grabbing her tools. As they work their magic, we catch up, with me telling them about how I returned home and to my nanny gig. The kids didn't see the show, but I had some interesting conversations with my bosses. Mindy especially wanted all the dirty details . . . and I do mean *dirty*.

"I really didn't know that she had such a naughty streak to her!" I remark, making Brad chuckle. "What?"

"Honey, I hate to tell you, but me and Mindy's sister Roxy go waaaaay back. I know all about Mindy's naughty side. Next time you see her, ask her if she's taken any dogs for walks on the beach recently."

I raise an eyebrow at the mysterious comment, but I just wave it off. I probably don't even want to know what that means. "Anyway, I took the opportunity, and the little bit of money I've made from the show, to return to school. It's a few nights per week, but I'm making great grades and should graduate with my teaching degree in less than two years since my previous classes counted. It's weird being the oldest in the class and having some level of recognition. Although with Season Two premiering, the other students have finally stopped asking me questions about the show."

"I bet," McKayla says. "By the way, I've got some news too. Well, we both do." She looks at Brad as they grab hands.

I laugh, holding up my hands "Please don't tell me you've fallen in love, because I'm not sure that's how this works. Although you would be the two most fabulous brides I've ever seen."

Brad grins and gives me a wink. "Oh, hell no, I am never marrying this salacious slut. No, girl, McKayla's my bitch and all, but she's not exactly sporting the right parts for me, if you know what I mean."

McKayla laughs and pats Brad on the butt. "Yeah, I think we get what you mean. You're not very subtle at all. But no . . . that's not what I was gonna say."

McKayla takes a big breath, then gushes out, "We're leaving the show. Brad and I, we're opening our own studio, be our own bosses and all. Some weddings, some contracts for fashion week or photo shoots, regular clientele of bottle blondes, and whoever else rolls in the door. Just striking out on our own." She smiles warmly at Brad. "Figured there was nobody else in the world I wanted to throw insults at all day."

I grin, getting out of my chair to hug them both again. "That's awesome! I'm so happy for you!" We hug as I thank them again for everything they did. "You know, I never really thanked you two lunatics for helping Hayden and me sneak around, holding me when I broke down, and helping me get back up again. I really hope you know that I love you both."

"Right back atcha, chica," McKayla says.

CHAPTER 28

HAYDEN

*E*mily and I sit down across the interviewer, the audience still applauding like crazy. The second episode of *Matchmaker: Season Two* just finished showing, and we're live in the studio. I know Emily's a little nervous, but that's okay. I saw Meredith as I walked onto set. As long as she's getting ratings ,she's not upset, and from what I've seen after two episodes, Cody's gonna do just fine. If anything, the scenes of his workout routine are probably going to be a hit with the ladies.

"Well, guys, it's so good to see you again," the host says, giving us a warm smile. "Last time you were here, you certainly surprised me."

"WE LOVE YOU GUYS!"

The host chuckles as Emily blushes and I grin. "Seems you have some fans."

We just smile. I mean, honestly, what do you say to that? The interview starts, with the host asking all the same questions about the Matchmaker show, and we recap the same answers we've always given. Maybe they're just doing it for the people who missed the first season—"Out now on streaming services!" the host reminds everyone—but in some ways, it feels like they're trying to catch us messing up. But our story is simply the truth. We fell in love in the midst of craziness, even with people engaged in heartless manipulation all around us.

"I know that the situation isn't quite what the show started off as," Emily says, downplaying that a bit now because the show doesn't want us to ruin the next season. Honestly, we just want them to stop calling us, so it's fine. "But I don't think it has anything to do with the show itself. I bet that Cody is going to have a great chance to find a beautiful young woman who's going to become to him what Hayden means to me."

"Speaking of becoming, what have you two been up to individually? Now, Hayden, I know you like to focus on Emily, but what about you? What have you been up to?"

I reach out and take Emily's hand. "Well, I was invited to Paris Fashion Week. We Skyped every night, but it was fun. Mostly, just me exhausted from the stress of backstage and her yawning from a full day with the kids and class notes." The audience chuckles. "But really, it's the best time of my life."

Emily grins. She knows that I've adjusted just fine to being a 'small town' sort of guy. "He's doing New York week too, and it's this summer, so I'll get to go with him. It'll be fun to sit in the audience and watch him. Show them your Zoolander Blue Steel look . . ."

I can't help it, I laugh and then give a serious look at the camera. It was a total joke, growing from a night playing poker, but I can see some of the ladies give their approval. Even the host melodramatically fans herself. They don't know the half of it though. That's just my 'working' face. I much prefer the personal photos, the ones we've snapped around town when I'm able to visit Emily and live with her, the ones where we go out to dinner or play with the kids as she takes care of them. Relaxing, I lean back, giving Emily's hand a squeeze. "Yeah, and while I'm in New York, I've got a big campaign to shoot for Diesel Jeans and then we'll see from there."

The host turns to Emily. "And you? So you're back to being a nanny?"

Emily shakes her head. "No, not exactly. The couple I work for, Mindy and Oliver, have practically made me part of their family. So I still look after their adorable children when they need me. Fewer hours than before, but it lets me complete my schooling, hopefully ready to teach in a couple of years when the kids are old enough to not really need me anymore. But they'll always be my heart."

"How about wedding bells and children of your own? Is that on the horizon at all?" the host asks, but before I can answer, Emily speaks up.

"It's still a little early for that. I need to finish school first for sure." Emily laughs, and I know she's trying to put the host off politely, but she's on my side. I pulled Meredith aside earlier today. I think it'll get me off Meredith's kill list, not that I really care.

I play along. "Yeah, maybe some day, like maybe . . ." I rise off the couch, dropping to one knee and holding out a ring. "Emily, no tricks, no surprises. Just you and me against the world. I love you. Through it all, that's always been true. I love you and I want to spend forever with you. Will you be my wife?"

The collective gasp from the audience almost sucks the air out of the room, and I know at least a million people are wondering if I've lost my damn mind. I mean, after all, the last time Emily was proposed to on live TV, things went . . . strangely.

I don't have a single doubt, though, as Emily looks in my eyes. "Hayden, um, for real? Yes, yes! Of course I'll marry you!"

The audience erupts with applause, rising to give us a standing ovation as we hug and kiss. After a moment, the host interrupts. "So does that mean we'll have a Matchmaker wedding special after all?"

I don't even look at the host, shaking my head as I look into my fiancé's eyes. "Absolutely not. This is all you get. Our wedding day is for us, family, and friends—no one else."

With another kiss overtaking us both, the host calls for a commercial break. Finally.

CHAPTER 29

EMILY

I feel nervous as we wait by the limo—a gift from Oliver—for Hayden's parents to arrive here at the airport. "When are they supposed to land?" I ask for what's probably the five hundredth time. "Is their flight late?"

Hayden, who's been the world's best fiancé this whole time, grins. "No, they're not late. Their Delta flight is supposed to have landed just five minutes ago. You know it takes a while to de-plane."

I sigh, rubbing at my arms. Since our very public and very unexpected engagement moment, I haven't really talked with Hayden's mom and dad, who've tried to give their son the space needed to do what needs done without being overbearing. "Hayden, are you sure that—"

"Stop," Hayden says, coming close and giving me a hug. "You're freaking out. Don't. You've talked to Mom and Dad over Skype a few times now. Besides, they don't allow torches and pitchforks on airplanes anymore."

"Very funny," I growl, punching him lightly in the ribs.

Hayden clutches at his side, moaning. "Starting the abuse early, I see. Oh, if I only knew about this dark side to you—"

"That he totally deserves," a gruff voice says behind us. "Why did you say yes to this ugly asshole anyway?"

I turn, seeing Hayden's dad, a bit taken aback at the comment. It's always seemed to me that Hayden's had a good relationship his parents. My fears evaporate in an instant, though, when I see Hayden embrace his dad, who I have to say for a man his age is still remarkably handsome. Hayden's mom embraces me, giving me a kiss on the cheek. "Welcome to the family, Emily."

"Thanks, Mrs. Bishop," I say, earning a tut from her.

"You know better than that. It's Vanessa," she says, correcting me. "I have to ask, though . . . a limo? Really?"

"When you're the nanny for a multi-millionaire, you sometimes get the good stuff." I laugh as the driver comes around and helps Vanessa and Mr. Bishop with their bags. We get in, and Hayden's dad leans back, impressed.

"Well, Hayden, you certainly picked the right girl," Gene, Hayden's father, says. "How in the hell did you manage to pull that one off?"

"I inherited my good looks and common sense from Mom and made sure to use as little of your DNA as possible," Hayden shoots back, Vanessa rolling her eyes. "Other than your hard head."

His mom leans over, whispering in my ear. "These two have been tossing insults back and forth ever since Hayden here first picked up a baseball."

"Is that so? Well, Hayden, I have to say, I'm damn proud of

you, Son. I have to admit, for a while there, I thought you'd end up with some inch-deep airhead who thinks slumming it is wearing only hundred-dollar shoes. So glad you caught this one here instead." He gestures to me with a tilt of his chin.

"Uh, excuse me?" I ask, raising an eyebrow. "I'm the one who stood up on live TV and told him I loved him when he was still being an ass to me. Pretty sure you should be proud of me."

Gene laughs, glancing at his son. "You'd better stay on your toes, Son. I was gonna tell her that if she ever needed help kicking your ass to give me a call. But I think she's got that handled already."

"Which reminds me," Vanessa says, "what happened to that plan you told us when you came home all heartbroken about telling Emily how you felt on the reunion show?"

"What can I say?" Hayden says, shrugging in an embarrassed way. "I didn't have a chance. I was going to, but Emily went into epic fire-breathing mode, and it worked out in the end for everyone. Like Tim Gunn says, make it work."

The church is perfect. Again, Oliver and Mindy went out of their way to give me what's perhaps the most epic wedding gift ever. I mean, who else has a chart topping singer perform at their reception? Sure, it's Mindy's sister, but it's also the one and only Roxy, and I'm just hoping I don't get too star-struck when I meet her.

"You ready?" Mindy asks me. She's serving as the matron of honor for my wedding, and maybe some folks would think it's weird to have your boss stand up with you, but we're basically family at this point and I'm damn proud to have her stand with me. I feel and look like a princess since McKayla and Brad flew in to do my hair and makeup—and be in the wedding party too.

"Totally," I reply, not nervous at all. This is Hayden, and there's nothing I want more in the world than to walk down the aisle and join the man of my dreams in matrimony. "When it was time for you and Oliver, did you have any doubts?"

Mindy chuckles, shaking her head. "Not a single one. Just a hint. When the doors open and you see him, don't go running down the aisle. You'd just have the kids chasing after you, and the photographer would probably shit himself."

I chuckle, nodding. "Okay, okay, I'll be all sweet and classical walking down the aisle. I'll save the running for the honeymoon."

The music starts, my father walking me down the aisle before joining Mom, who's sitting in the front row with a good pile of tissues already crumpled up beside her. The ceremony starts, and I have a hard time taking my eyes off Hayden, who's the most handsome man in the entire world in his tuxedo. I'm sure I mumble my way through my vows, barely focusing until it's time for the rings. Watching the simple platinum band slip onto my finger and then putting its partner on Hayden's, everything feels surreal. It doesn't really set in until our kiss. Like every kiss with Hayden, it's intense, but there's an added element to this one that sears it into my mind and soul. We're interrupted by the minister, who coughs lightly when I realize we've gone from a simple 'wedding kiss' to full-on snogging.

"Sorry," I say, earning a small laugh from the guests. Leah, Mindy's daughter, is blushing while Mindy's giving me a big thumbs-up. In the back, I see McKayla holding up both hands, her version of saying it was a perfect ten.

Retreating from the church, we're in the limo heading for the reception when Hayden turns and kisses me again. "You look amazing."

"You have no idea how sexy you look in that," I reply, reaching down and cupping his cock through his pants. "What do you say we skip the reception and steer this thing right to the airport?"

"Yeah, right," Hayden jokes, pulling me into his lap and lifting the poufy skirt and helping me straddle him. "We're going to the resort Oliver owns with his brother, remember? We skip the reception, and we're going to have that whole damn crew knocking down our door twelve hours after we get there."

I chuckle, leaning forward and kissing my husband. Hayden trails his lips along my neck, taking advantage of the strapless build of the dress to leave burning lines of passion on my skin. I gasp, then giggle as I straddle his waist. I feel the thick bulge of his cock through his pants and my hips take over. I rub my panty-covered pussy over him, heat and wetness quickly soaking the thin silk. The limo suddenly jerks, and I stop, laughing and giggling in terror and heat. "What are we doing?"

Hayden doesn't stop, reaching down to pull one of the cups of my gown down and capture my nipple, making me gasp. He nibbles and sucks strongly, overpowering any resistance I have. Letting go of my nipple, Hayden reaches between my legs, tugging my panties to the side while growling in my ear, "I can't wait to be inside my beautiful wife."

His deep need wipes away the last traces of hesitation inside me, and I kiss him fiercely, lifting my hips to let Hayden undo his pants. Just as I feel the head of his cock press against my aching pussy lips, there's a knock on the divider screen, and McKayla's voice comes over the intercom. "Hey, guys, not to interrupt, but we're gonna be at the reception soon. How long should I tell the photographer to wait? He's ranting on the phone about missing the sunset for your pics. So finish up. You've got five minutes after we get there before I snatch the keys from the driver and I'm coming in."

I hear the intercom click off and I giggle as Hayden looks at me. Thankfully, we're both so close. "Five minutes?"

"And traffic," Hayden reminds me. He pulls me down, filling me with one long thrust until he's balls-deep and my eyes are rolling back in my head. "I can work with that."

"You'd better not leave me hanging," I warn him as I squeeze my pussy around his cock. "Your honeymoon is not going to be pleasant if you do."

"I promise," he says as he lifts me up and starts thrusting. "You're gonna scream my name."

There's no time for slow strokes or tenderness, but we don't need it. That'll come tonight after we get to the hotel on the way to our honeymoon. This is about animal need, and Hayden's cock hammers deep inside me with powerful strokes. I ride him like a bucking bronco, bracing my hands against the roof of the limo to prevent knocking myself dizzy.

It's naughty, sexy, and arousing as hell, looking down into my husband's eyes while wearing my wedding dress and feeling his cock rubbing deep inside me. My clit rubs against the inner lining of my skirt as I roll my hips faster and harder, both of us gasping. "Fuck me, Hayden . . . oh, fuck, baby, it's so fucking good."

Dimly, in the one percent of my mind that isn't obsessed with being fucked silly, I'm aware of the limo coming to a stop, but it doesn't matter. I'm so close, my fingers are clawing at the roof I so need the release. Hayden is gasping too, grunting like a wild animal as he pumps his cock up into me hard as he can. "Not much longer . . ."

I scream, the trembles starting in the balls of my feet before rolling up my legs and through my spine before everything drops like an elevator with no brakes. I come, the explosion ripping from the very center of my body to rocket up my chest, through my swelling heart to pour out of my mouth in one long, single word. "Hayden!"

Hayden growls my name one last time before he plunges himself all the way inside me and I feel his seed fill me. We've been 'unsafe' for a while now, but this time feels different, maybe because we're man and wife. The power of our orgasms seem to be a testament to the bond between us and the power of what we have overcome.

I gasp, sweat running down my face as I look into Hayden's eyes. There's another knock on the divider, and it's McKayla again. "Well?"

"One minute," Hayden says with a laugh. "We're coming!" The intercom clicks off, and he laughs before looking up at me. "Well, I kept my promise."

I lean forward, kissing his lips lightly. "That you did. Now, let's go take some pictures."

We adjust our clothing as best we can and get out of the limo. As we open the door, Brad tsks us, looking me up and down.

"Damn, girl, you are gonna look freshly fucked in your wedding pics. Let me touch up your lipstick at least. And you, go wash the shine off the front of your damn tux. I can't trust my hands around that area."

I grin, not giving a shit about the pics as long as Hayden is in them with me. "Okay, okay, we'll behave."

Hayden grins, adjusting his tux jacket. "For now."

EPILOGUE

EMILY - 18 MONTHS LATER

I glance at the clock, seeing that it's nearly six thirty, but I'm not worried. Gina's father gave me a call before lunch, and he'll be here soon. I just wish he'd hurry up. I love my work, but tonight's special.

"Mrs. Bishop?" Gina asks me as I click *Save* on the last file I'm doing today. "When are you coming back?"

I look down at my belly, rubbing the swelling bulge underneath my t-shirt, and smile. "Don't worry, I plan on still coming to school. But I'm going to have to take it easy for a while. You don't know how hard it is keeping up with you and twenty of your classmates."

Gina, who just turned eight and is an only child, has shown a massive amount of fascination with my pregnancy. More than once, she's come up during breaks in class to touch my belly. "But you've got months before the baby comes. My mommy said it's not coming until Christmas break."

"True," I admit, "but the doctor told me that it'd be better if I kept to just doing administrative work. I'm sure Miss Richards will do a great job of teaching you guys. She taught elementary school for five years before coming here."

She nods and goes back to her homework. Starting a private school has been the challenge of my lifetime, and it would have been impossible without the help of my friends in town. Whether it was the generous contribution from my wealthy former employers or the support from my friend Cassie and her husband Caleb that helped me refurbish the old building near the university to bring it up to code, Blue Water Academy was just a pipe dream without their help.

And Hayden. My beloved husband has used his own rising fame to bring in support. You'd be shocked at the amount of cookies you can sell at a bake sale when you have a man as good-looking as him pitching them. With him using his fame to only take big-money modeling contracts, he's home more than most husbands. In the past year, he's been away from home only three weeks total. Hard, but when I consider that we get to spend twenty-four hours a day together the other forty-nine weeks . . . I'll take it.

"Mrs. Bishop?" Gina asks again, interrupting my thoughts as I look around the room. We've got four classrooms now, a kindergarten and three rooms divided into two-year combined classes. With a small gym, a bus, and a big play-ground in the back, we're already looking at having to expand in the next two years to deal with the number of applications we're getting.

"Yes, Gina?" I reply, turning away from the class picture on the wall. "Are you getting hungry?"

"A little," she admits, "but I had a question. Mommy says you are Cinderella. What does she mean? You don't have a pumpkin carriage."

I laugh softly. I guess the title does fit, in a certain way. "Your mommy is just saying that she thinks I'm lucky to have found my husband. I'll let you in on a secret . . . I think your mommy's right."

There's a knock on the classroom door and I look to see Gina's father on the security monitor. She sees, too, and goes to the back, getting her backpack. "See you later, Mrs. Bishop."

"Have a good weekend, Gina," I reply, walking her to the door. Opening the door, I see Gina give her father a big hug, kissing him on the cheek. "Thanks for the call earlier, Mr. Farnham."

Her father shakes his head, smiling. "Thank you for being so helpful, Emily. I'm sorry mine and my wife's jobs make us late sometimes, but I know my little girl is safe while she's here."

"How is Dr. Farnham anyway?" I ask. "Working night shift?"

"Life of an ER doc," he says with a shrug. "She'll be off second shift in three weeks and back to days. Speaking of the hospital, you make sure you take care of that little one inside you. Have you found out if it's a boy or a girl yet?"

I shake my head, knowing that there's a betting pool going around the school and among the PTA for whether I have a boy or a girl and the delivery date. "Nope, not yet. I'm hoping for a girl, and Hayden wants a boy. What can you say?"

"You can say that I'm a monster daddy who wants a little boy who'll play for the Yankees," a low, amused voice says from behind Mr. Farnham. I can't help but grin as Hayden steps forward from the parking lot. I hadn't expected him back until tomorrow.

"Hey, beautiful."

I step out, hugging him as Gina and her father wave their goodbyes. I feel that stomach-dropping thrill just like I always do as he picks me up and carries me back inside the classroom. "How'd the shoot for Diesel go?"

"Smooth as silk," Hayden says, kissing my neck. "All I had to do was think of you, and they said I had the 'male sex gaze' down to a science. And everyone's cool with the fact that I'm not doing shoots for the next six months. I'm gonna be a stay-at-home Daddy for the foreseeable future."

Hayden's lips trail down my neck to suck and nip just below my jaw, sending thrills through my body. "Hey . . ." I half moan, stepping back. "Isn't this against school rules?"

Hayden gives me a naughty smile and turns around, locking the classroom door. "Yeah," he growls, picking up a jar of red tempera paint that we use for art projects. "Here we go."

"What are you doing?" I giggle as Hayden picks up a paint-brush, his eyes sparkling as he looks at me. "Oh, hell, no. Hayden Bishop, I swear, if you—"

Hayden stops and pulls his shirt open, exposing his chiseled torso. I know it's stupid, and he can turn me on with a glance anytime, but when Hayden has to get a little more ripped for a photo shoot for the 'stud' fashion lines . . . yeah, I got pregnant after a particularly active weekend when he was prepping for a photo shoot for Under Armour.

Now, I just watch in horny fascination as he whips his shirt off and takes the top off the paint, dipping the brush in before painting a line down his chest. I follow it down from the swell of his pecs and down over the washboard of his abs before he stops as he hits his belt. "Well, teacher? You want to help me with my art project?"

To hell with it. There's a few benefits to being one of the co-owners and administrative staff of the school, and that includes being able to break the rules when I want. I reach for the buttons on my blouse, biting my lip as my heart speeds up and the familiar but always delicious tingle starts between my legs and around my nipples. "I was thinking," I reply as I reach the swell of my belly, "that maybe we could make this a partner project?"

Hayden lets out an aroused growl as I finish unbuttoning my blouse and slide it from my shoulders to drop to the floor. "I think I want to paint *you* now."

I smile and reach between my breasts to the clasp of my bra. "Just one thing . . . nothing on the tender parts. They say that stuff's non-toxic, but I don't want to lick paint off your cock."

Hayden grins and dips the brush into the paint again. "So we have some fun painting, then we go home and—"

"And have fun washing it all off," I agree, unhooking my bra. "Think of it as your homework."

Hayden steps forward, his voice lowering to a sexy growl. "I love school."

So do I.

Have you read all the current books in this series?

Irresistible Bachelor **Series (Interconnecting standalones):**
Anaconda ‖ Mr. Fiance ‖ Heartstopper

**Stud Muffin ǁ Mr. Fixit ǁ Matchmaker
Motorhead ǁ Baby Daddy**

**Join my mailing list and receive 2 FREE ebooks! You'll
also be the first to know of new releases, sales, and
giveaways.**

EXCERPT: MOTORHEAD

BY LAUREN LANDISH

EVAN

I rub at my temples, washing down the second of the damn horse pills the VA gave me for bad times with a swig of coffee and wincing. It's already been a shitty day, and it's only eleven A.M. Even on good days, I'm getting no more than four hours of sleep a night, and I know my caffeine habit is getting the best of me. But I didn't sleep at all last night, not that that's anything new since I got back from my last tour and the nightmares started.

Well, nightmares might be putting it lightly since the dreams that plague me are more like sleeping reenactments of the worst moments of my life. I see them all the time, the ghostly images that I know are supposed to just be in my head but sometimes seem so damn real at two in the morning. I rolled out of bed at seven simply because I couldn't stand to lie around anymore. I felt like an extra in *The Walking Dead*, but I sucked it up and drove on, as we used to say. I took a shower, skipping the shave today because fuck it, and got ready to hit the day because that's what you do when you're responsible for helping out at a family business that provides both a needed distraction and the funds to survive.

What you don't do is what too many of my buddies have— fall into drinking, drugs, and for some of them, eating the end of a pistol barrel. I can't call them pussies. Some of those guys were the hardest-core motherfuckers any man could hope to meet. But that's not me. I'm not looking for congrat- ulations, but damn if I couldn't use a little slack today.

Not that I've gotten any. As soon as I walked into the shop, my brother TJ started giving me shit about not pulling my weight when I drag-ass in an hour late and run off potential clients with my lack of customer service skills. "You can't just get by with being good with a wrench, goddammit!" he yelled at me. "You have to actually talk to people!"

He's probably right, but the last thing I need is my little brother telling me how to live, especially when he's had a cushy life here at home, never having to battle a damn thing other than some nerves when he asked his flavor of the week out for a drink or a fuck, her choice.

So I'm already near my boiling point when I walk outside to grab another coffee and a cigarette to clear my head so I can tackle the engine rebuild on my schedule today. It's not a bad one. Old GM small blocks are pieces of cake compared to European builds, but I want to be able to focus, and that means coffee. I just step out the door when I see some chick damn near lying on my bike.

Before I can even think, all of my anger from the morning boils over as I charge forward like a raging bull, exploding from deep in my chest. "What the fuck are you doing to my motorcycle?"

I see her jerk back, startled by the noise. Who does she think she is? Hands off my baby. I built this cycle from the frame up, and nobody, not even my brother, gets to touch it without my say-so.

The woman turns to face me, a placating smile already on her red-painted lips. "I'm so sorry! It's just such a gorgeous machine, I couldn't help myself." She dips her chin and pulls up one side of her smile a bit more, her head tilted slightly, and I can tell she's used the practiced pose to get her way more than once. Considering the smooth, creamy skin she's showing off under the tied-up t-shirt she's wearing, she probably doesn't have to ask twice either.

I huff, but that act isn't going to work on me. "It is gorgeous. Know what else it is?" I wait a half-beat, but before she can even open her mouth, I answer my own question. "Mine. Back. The. Fuck. Up."

She's taken aback by my vehemence, her eyes going wide as her full lips round, taking in a gasp of air. She is hot, not like most chicks I see around here. I mean, she's rocking metallic pink hair like it's nobody's business, and the jeans she's wearing do look natural on a bike like mine, but that's only if invited first. She stutters and swings off my bike, letting me see the rest of her, and she's no less hot in that tight t-shirt that shows off a front side nearly as curvy as her backside. "Again, I'm sorry. I knocked on the door to ask but nobody answered—"

"So you knew that it wasn't right but went ahead and touched my bike anyway? Yeah, you sound really sorry, Princess."

I can see the switch flip in her eyes instantly as she goes from nicely trying to apologize to nuclear. Guess she's got a button to push.

"I'm not a damn princess, asshole," she fires back, turning and jabbing a finger at me. "I just wanted to take a picture with your bike for our new salon. I'm sorry I touched it. Obviously, that's my bad. But you don't have to be so fucking rude."

As she rants, I'm suddenly struck by how the fire crackles in her wild eyes and the flush moves down her cheeks. She's gesturing all around with her hands like some caricature, pointing at me, the bike, and vaguely across the street. She's *cute* when she's pissed.

I can't help but laugh, but it's a snarky dark chuckle that she takes as my still being rude, though it wasn't really my intention. She plants her balled-up fists on her hips while the guy, who's looking like he wants to be anywhere *but* here, shakes in his overly tight khakis, holding his camera like a shield.

My eyes are mostly filled with the pixie in front of me that's about to go apeshit on me. "What? What the fuck are you laughing at?"

I can't help it, her boldness makes me laugh even harder. "Did you really just try to tell me that you're not a Princess? Have you seen yourself? Pink nails flicking all about, and makeup done like you're in a damn movie? And that hair? You look like a Powerpuff Girl or something. You're a walking, talking Pink Barbie Princess, honey."

Her voice drops to a throaty growl, and I know for sure that she doesn't appreciate being called Princess. A part of me that isn't pissed off and caught up in my throbbing headache sort of wonders why. "Don't call me Princess. If you want to address me, my name is McKayla, but I think we'd be better off if you just didn't call me anything, ever again. Sorry for touching your precious bike, asshole."

With a hair flip, McKayla pivots in her heels and stomps away. She's obviously pissed as fuck, flipping me off as she talks faintly to herself about what a jerk I am. But with every stomp, her ass bounces and sways, creating a sexy image if I ever saw one.

I cross my arms and watch her for a moment, one corner of my lips sneaking up just a bit until I feel eyes on me. I realize that the guy is still there, his polka-dot bowtie somehow adding that touch of absolute ridiculous unreality that makes me know for sure this isn't some waking nightmare. I'd never imagine this. He's watching me watch her, and I raise an eyebrow at him, not saying a word.

"So. That's McKayla and I'm Brad," he says in a lispy voice that certainly advertises which team he swings for. "We're the owners of the new Triple B Salon across the street. And who did we have the pleasure of meeting today?"

I nearly gape in disbelief. Shit. They're literally my new fucking neighbors. Of course they are, because that's how fucked up my life is. TJ's gonna kill me. With a hearty sigh, I look up to the sky, silently cursing whatever joke fate is trying to play on me.

Looking back at Brad, I relent and offer a hand. He shakes, and despite his effeminate aura, he's got a good grip to him. "I'm Evan Hardwick. My brother TJ and I own this garage. Looks like we're neighbors. Welcome to the neighborhood. But don't touch my bike."

Brad nods, taking his hand back. "Understood. Loud and

clear. FYI, I'm the nice one. You've heard the expression 'a bark worse than the bite'?"

I nod, thinking I know where this is headed. "She's feisty but a little playful puppy inside?"

Brad shakes his head, surprising me. "McKayla's got a hell of a bark, but her bite is even worse."With a hum of disapproval, he gives me a look and then offers a little finger wave and sashays across the street toward the new storefront. I watch him walk in the door and then hop on my bike. I light it up with a grumble of the engine, the aggressive snarl mirroring my mood perfectly. I pull away from the shop, gunning it as I turn a half-circle and double-shift as I pass the salon window, the engine going from a howl to a full scream. Hidden behind sunglasses, I cut my eyes over to the salon. As I pass, I tell myself that I won that little battle of the day as I fly out to the highway, needing the wind in my face to let go of the shitty morning.

Want to read the rest? Get it HERE or visit my website at www.laurenlandish.com

ABOUT THE AUTHOR

Join my mailing list and receive 2 FREE ebooks! You'll also be the first to know of new releases, sales, and giveaways.

Connect with Lauren Landish
www.laurenlandish.com
admin@laurenlandish.com

***Irresistible Bachelor* Series (Interconnecting standalones):**
Anaconda ‖ Mr. Fiance ‖ Heartstopper
Stud Muffin ‖ Mr. Fixit ‖ Matchmaker
Motorhead ‖ Baby Daddy